HOW
WINTER
BEGAN

Flyover Fiction Series

SERIES EDITOR
Ron Hansen

HOW
WINTER
BEGAN

Stories

Joy Castro

UNIVERSITY OF NEBRASKA PRESS

LINCOLN AND LONDON

Library of Congress
Cataloging-in-Publication Data
Castro, Joy.
[Short stories. Selections]
How winter began: stories / Joy Castro.
pages; cm.—(Flyover fiction)
ISBN 978-0-8032-7660-4 (pbk.: alk. paper)
ISBN 978-0-8032-8479-1 (EPUB)
ISBN 978-0-8032-8480-7 (MOBI)
ISBN 978-0-8032-8481-4 (PDF)
I. Title.
PS3603.A888A6 2015   813'.6—dc23
2015018230

Set in Garamond Premier Pro by M. Scheer.

For Grey

It must be so lovely to be always
like a balcony, all empty
and carefree, only looking!

ROSARIO CASTELLANOS,
Balún Canán

CONTENTS

HOW
WINTER
BEGAN

A Notion I Took

I jumped into the San Antonio River once, for a hundred dollars. After I got pregnant and had to quit dancing, I worked nights waiting tables at The Bayous down on the Riverwalk. The night I jumped, Marisa was still nursing, and my breasts were fat and swollen with it. The belly left was nothing, hidden under the black apron we all wore for pens and the money.

Eleven o'clock, we were still turning tables. *CATS* was at the Majestic, and we had a special menu to catch the people coming out late. They flooded the lobby, gabbing and impatient, all excited with their fancy clothes and the opinions they were saying. Maybe a hundred of them, and the manager freaking out, *we're out of this, we're out of that, you bus table seven right now or you're fired,* and the busboy getting stoned in the cooler when you go in to find more lemons. Fuck, what a night.

A four-top of men from Tennessee kept messing with me—business guys, not theater people. They were in their forties, fat, flush with ego and big gold watches in the candlelight, proud over some triumph they kept lifting their bottles to. Every time I crossed the patio with more salsa or another round, it would be something: "Baby, are all the girls here as fine—" and that kind of shit. Come to Texas, play cowboy for a week. But one thing led to another until I was saying the things I say when men flirt. Bold, dumb things. Then it was happening: a hundred lay flat on the table, the river stretched out like a grin, and I was giving my apron to another girl to hold. I smiled and waved from the edge of the safe cement while the whole restaurant looked on, holding its breath.

Standing there, I knew the plunge was only half of what they wanted: to see a woman do something crazy, maybe get fired, even—the power of their money that could work other people like puppets. That, I knew all about. And the other half I knew about, too: the girlie show when I'd get out, black hair streaming and sticking, wet brown flesh gleaming silver, mouth all vulnerable, opened for air, the white shirt transparent, clinging, showing the black bra, the full ripe slope of the breasts, nipples prodding, the nursing pads' little white circles the only surprise. The whole restaurant would gape.

Standing on the edge, I could hear already the sudden clapping when I climbed out, see the hot glazed rove of male eyes, the tight smiles of women applauding to show their dates they weren't bothered, of course not, why should they be? The laughter and looks that would follow me as I strode between the tables to the four Tennessee men and took my hundred. In my bra I would tuck it. And they'd roar.

The other waiters would look pissed, and the ratlike manager would write me up, furious, fidgeting with loose fabric at the knee of his khakis. But the owner wouldn't fire me. She'd shake her head, smiling, and wave him off, privately pleased that her restaurant might get known as a place where things happened, where things could get wild, where a waitress might jump in the river, who knew? Anything to stand out in a tourist zone as safe and planned as Disney.

The four Tennessee men would get a story to take back with them about those crazy big-titty Mexican girls down in San Antone: just like a border town, man, anything for a buck. You go there yourself. You try it. And me, I would get to take the money and the rest of the night off, listen to the manager bitch, go home to my apartment where my mom would freak out and switch back and forth between yelling at me, "My God, Iréne! What is this? What are you doing with yourself for God's sake?" and telling me all about her TV show. Finally she'd go.

It would be quiet, then, just me and Marisa. I'd shower and scrub off the scum and toxic waste, soaping and resoaping the nipples to make sure, and I'd put the hundred in the Catholic school jar under the bed and nurse Marisa, the whole time thinking, *Who the hell knows anything about me?* until we fell asleep in the big bed together. I could see it all happening like that as I stood on the edge in the dark.

I turned from them then, leaping and arching, flying for a second and then falling, falling through air and falling in water, the lukewarm rush of it filling my ears with silence, blotting out the clatter of dishes and quick kitchen disputes, the fake smiles at the table and the things you say to make people with money give some to you. All of it, gone. Just a rush of soft silence, the slippery liquid the same warmth as my skin holding me as I swept through in a shallow arch. It's a canal, after all, made for drainage and boatloads of white people. But deep enough. I felt my body slowing. *This water is filthy*, I thought as I kept going down, and I kept my eyes closed against it. *So filthy and polluted they dump dye in to make it blue for the tourists.* And I thought as I sank how soft the words sounded: *filthy, polluted.* I tried to think, *No real water is turquoise,* as its silk slid over me and my own weight pulled me down. *It's only filth, with color added,* I tried to think in the dark smooth quiet, but all I could feel was its pull like the pull of a soft door opening.

How to Warp Your Kid

When he comes home from Montessori claiming life's not fair because girls are luckier than boys, do a double-take. Refrain from saying that your own twenty-seven years of existence have not borne this out. Ask him what he means.

When he says that girls get to wear pants *or* skirts, while boys can only wear pants, and that's not fair, say, "Ah." Nod sagely. You're in graduate seminars on deconstruction, feminist theory, postcolonialism. You read Foucault. You can handle this one. This one's easy compared to those *Why is the sky blue?* questions that strain your memory of Physics in the Fine Arts, which you took instead of a lab science because you are intellectually lazy and cutting fetal things makes you sick.

Explain cultural hegemony to your five-year-old. In short words. He grasps it; he's bright. At two, he squeezed the huggable stuffed globe your friend Margaret gave him, pointed to India, and said, "That's where they don't eat hamburgers." He has never eaten a hamburger. He has remained a strict vegetarian even after you met a guy—at the health food store, no less—who took you to New Orleans for a weekend where you tumbled off the wagon into platterfuls of seafood and you have never been able to clamber entirely back on. Your son is nobler than you. He is pure. In his soul, equations balance. Your variables careen all over the place; you cannot seem to solve for y. You are messed up, a fuckup, a single mother at twenty-seven paying your son's Montessori bill with your own student loans.

So your five-year-old starts a club to end cultural hegemony and paints a sign and establishes club headquarters deep inside the Ligustrum bush, but none of the married-student-housing kids will join. Only his best friend agrees to humor him, and soon The Club to End Cultural Hegemony is merely an elaborate front for a Lego-playing operation.

Take a fiction-writing class when your academic load gets too heavy. Hand in a story to your workshop called "Find the Thinly Veiled Ex-Husband." Open the story with the disclaimer, "Any resemblance to any real person, living or dead, who has totally fucked me over & skipped town & refuses to pay child support & whose sorry ass I can't afford to sue, is completely coincidental." Get called angry. Be told your work is highly derivative and imitative of somebody, they can't think who. Graduate, get a job, get called lucky, move across the country.

When your son is thirteen, show him the video your estranged father sends of Disney World and Epcot, where he has promised to take him for a grandpa-grandson vacation. Watch it together on the couch, holding hands. Wish you could afford to take him anywhere. Wish your father had taken you anywhere; be grateful on behalf of grandchildren everywhere for the mellowing effects of andropause. Collapse keening on the kitchen floor when you receive, over the phone from a stranger, the news that your father has died from a coronary infarction. Stay there sobbing in a heap while your son stands above you, twisting his hands, saying, "Mama?" See his scared eyes. Recollect yourself. Comfort him. Say you are sorry about Disney World.

Get tenure when your son is seventeen. Buy a little bungalow in the neighborhood he likes. Above the mantelpiece, hand-paint *Idleness is the root of all love.* Spend the summer stripping the floors and painting the walls. Knowing he will only be there for a year, paint his room with him, coating its walls in the strange slate blue he picks. Do the white trim very slowly. When you finish, sit on the floor in the center of the room with your arm around him. Feel like you're inside a big Wedgwood ashtray.

Get bladder cancer. Cry in private. Make a will. Break the news to him. Hold him. Make a joke out of it. When the phone rings, say, "Would you get that? I have cancer." Laugh goofily and loud together and don't meet each other's eyes. "You take out the trash. I have cancer." Have surgery, get chemo, puke a lot, wear a wig. Recover. Feel irrevocably fragile. Obsessively inspect your pee.

Buy him a car that's safer and better than yours, a used Volvo with every safety feature in the world. Teach him to drive. Wonder where his father is. Try not to get Chinese takeout or pizza too many nights a week.

All year, drive him to every college he wants to visit. Sing John Denver tunes in the car until he begs you to please shut up and puts buds in his ears and disappears from you for sixty or seventy miles at a stretch.

On campuses, hang back. Let him ask the questions. Do not ask about curriculum or campus safety or the accident rate on the rock-climbing wall. Do not refer to him as *my baby*. Do not strike up friendly chitchat with the admissions officers or the professors or the student tour guides. Tell yourself, *This is his show.* Take Ativan. On the drive home, resolve not to pump him, however subtly, for his opinions. Remind yourself that to point out strengths and weaknesses is a doomed enterprise, sure to backfire. Fail. Irritate him.

At his high school graduation, cry. Sit alone. Do not approach your ex-husband and his new wife, who looks twelve, who have flown in from California, where you did not know they lived.

Do not comment when their only graduation gift is a plastic box of color-coordinated office supplies.

That summer, learn to kayak. Learn to sail. Take cello lessons. Learn to play your son's favorite video games, so you can sit on the couch together. Do not comment about the levels of violence or negative depictions of women. On the evenings he is out with friends, which are most evenings, learn to cook for one. Buy the cheerful cookbook: *Cooking for One!* Try not to feel entirely frantic as you acquire new interests, new hobbies, new friends, in the hope that they will fill up the time when he is gone. Learn astronomy. Borrow a colleague's telescope and spend long hours gazing at faraway bright things.

Walk back to your car from the dorm that is now his home. Get in and drive away fast, not glancing in the rearview mirror, not once. Turn on NPR and handle it all just perfectly, until "La Vie en Rose" comes on, and you have to pull off the highway and into the parking lot of a Cracker Barrel and put your head on your folded arms on the steering wheel, because you have always been a sucker for Piaf's frail warble of joy. Hate NPR for betraying you this way. Do not look up as the people walk by. When the tap comes on your window from the concerned elderly couple, do not raise your head. Just wave them away with your hand.

Other Women's Jewels

She wasn't Indian in the first place, which is to say she wasn't Native American, as she'd learned to call it rather quickly when she'd gotten the job. Or better yet: to say Zuni, Hopi, Pueblo— just as she'd say French, German, Italian. In an upscale store you used the upscale terms, or you risked putting off the upscale clients who drifted from boutique to boutique in the upscale little mall.

It was odd how things had turned out. All her life she'd wanted to be the girl in the Wrigley's commercial, skating swimming riding a horse, minty and gleaming with light. In school she'd switched her name from Lourdes to Liz, but no one had seemed to notice. Years of flamenco and tap, and still it was, "Well, I just don't know. We'll have to see," until she'd done three back-handsprings in a row and they'd had to put her on the squad at last—with awkward pretty blond girls who couldn't do the splits.

Odd. Because when the manager of Native Jewels had looked her over, it was her soft straight black hair falling to the small of her back, it was her smooth nut-colored skin and night eyes, and not the grade point average or abandoned scholarships typed neatly on her little résumé that made him hire her.

"But I'm Mexican," she'd said softly. "Chicana. Not Indian."

"Well, right," he'd answered, straightening his tie, his glance drawn to some movement at the front of the shop, "but you don't have to mention it to the customers, do you?" He'd cleared his throat and smiled. "You look Native American, and that's what's important. Native American enough," he'd said reassuringly, and so she got the best-paying job she'd been able to find, what with only two years of college and an eight-month-old baby back home at her mother's apartment.

She borrowed money from her mother's night-nurse wages to buy a week's worth of clothes—skirts and blouses which could be matched and then re-matched the following week and perhaps no one would notice until she got her first check and could buy a few more things. Her mother's old earrings and necklaces were fashionable again, fashionable enough to borrow, and the manager had said that after three months if she worked out all right then she could choose a couple of the low-ticket items for herself as long as she wore them in the store regularly. And a 10 percent discount on everything else.

It wasn't bad, really. She liked memorizing the stories. Each piece of jewelry had a backstory, a small printed card tucked into the box beneath the velvet. What the little figures meant: that's what the customers always asked first, and she always answered correctly: "This one symbolizes fertility and wisdom," or "This one means that the wearer has a deep heart," or that "the wearer has an old soul," or "a kind spirit," or "great vision," and the women would clutch the little pendants or bracelets or earrings and murmur, "Oh yes, perfect," and reach for their wallets, although Liz often read the cards suspiciously, wondering if perhaps the tiny silver man brandishing a spear might not really be crying something quite different. When business was slow, she would sit on the deerhide-covered stool and imagine herself telling the handbagged patrons her own explanations and then watching them shriek aghast and faint to the woven sisal.

But there were other things to memorize, too, the magical names of gems like secret charms from a fairy tale: topaz, turquoise, amethyst. She checked out a gemology book from the library so she could tell the customers how each stone formed beneath the earth, which chemicals composed it, which forces melded its hot liquid into shape. Her boss was impressed and thought perhaps they could move that three-month review up to two months, and the clients loved it. They loved to hear about the thousands of years of heat and pressure that would dangle from their lobes. Heat. Pressure. She could almost feel them contract with pleasure when she said it.

And the tribes of course she knew, even down to the reservation where each piece was made, each with its own certification number promising that its maker was a genuine full-blooded Navajo or Cherokee or Hopi. That seemed to excite the women too: the authenticity, that this particular jewel and its setting had been shaped for them by a real person (Liz noticed they always said "he"), a person living in perhaps a very hot and dry place, perhaps in a home without running water or electricity even, a person who sweated in the sun and bent metals with his hands and perhaps ate food cooked over an open fire. And that their money was going there, helping that good native man who toiled in the heat and the dust and perhaps without any shirt on: that was surely a thrilling and commendable thing.

No, it wasn't a bad job, and they weren't bad women, not bad women at all, no more than the people whose bedpans her mother changed and cleaned were bad people. The way they said to her mother, "Clara, can you hurry up, there's a good girl," only made you see how needy they were, how dependent really, as her mother said. And actually they were often very nice, sharing chocolates when they had some left, or letting Clara have their bouquets when they started to fade, because they knew she made little pictures and bookmarks with pressed flowers.

They knew it from the times when they were lonely and wanted someone to talk to, wanted to know about her life.

All around the shared apartment, little withered flowers hung: over the sofa, over the kitchen table, on the wall above the toilet. Pressed petals from other women's bouquets, glued slowly by Clara's knotted hands onto scraps of leftover cards.

One evening Liz came home tired from work and found a new picture, dahlia petals and periwinkles flattened against the cream-colored back of an old greeting card, hanging above the baby's little crib. And she couldn't have said why she moved so quickly, with a swift convulsive clutch, why she swept her daughter out from under it, up out of the blankets, and carried her rushingly into the lamplight.

When the baby awoke and gazed quietly, half smiling, Liz sank into the rocker, stroking the soft light curls back from the tiny forehead with a quick soothing stroke until she felt herself gradually grow calmer. *Mi hija, mi querida*, she sang to the baby in a low voice, rocking her, gazing into the wet blue blossoms of her eyes.

Giving Jewel Away

"The jewel of the first water, the face of the sleeping child." I don't know where the lines came from, where I'd read, "the nipple of the beloved wife, the beatific spine," but they stuck with me, and I wished I knew who'd written them—then, in the fifth month, when the sonogram promised a girl. Swimmer, quiet turtle turning over, guiding and twirling me through a new dance, a fertile glide. I practiced saying goodbye.

What bloodstorms blossom in a belly, in a woman's unsure heart? Of course they looked the best on paper, but to imagine them carrying my bones away?—The bindings in the hospital, the pain, and the breasts which are now softer to no purpose.

I learned that mine was not the first illicit product of a love affair so named. My own minister was a braver, better man, but I raved like any Addie in her coffin, drinking and vomiting up the pain for months, the only anesthetic for the treasure I'd set free, leaving my own self the one buried.

Babygirl, little sister, tiny mother, you birthed out of your own birth a torn creature left heaving in your wake, rawborn and blood-drenched, but with none of the birth smear to rub into my skin, nothing to protect from the flaying of the air, the mockery of the day, the kindness from friends who thought they understood. The depths I surged to, the ugly fires I kindled and put out with my wrists, all hunting a little peace of mind.

And always of course the stupid, pointless lacerations of wondering. *Are you the Christmas angel on the wheelbarrow of cut grass, a cornflower stabbed into your dark hair? (Is it dark?) Are you the girl cross-legged on the front porch lacing potholders on a plastic loom? Do you sing to yourself, and once in a while stare off, forgetting to weave, forgetting the song? Can you dial 911 if something happens and nobody's there? How does she hold you and rock you when you get the littlegirl blues?* The wondering about you that does not stop. The longing, the weeping, the surgery of tears.

Chanter, whisperer, there's a brave gaping hole in my chest where you used to live. I was just an apartment for you, a motel on the highway. A lifeboat until you could climb out, haul yourself up the ladder to a worthy ship, one that could carry you and keep carrying you to dry land.

Did the Black Hills' old-growth heal me? Not on the sweet blue gasp of your umbilical cord it didn't. Released from the weight of you, a helium balloon let go, I should have floated up through ponderosa needles to a sky-blue sky. But I lumbered, heavy and handicapped like a horse that runs too fast for the stakes. Timber-criers sized me up and disdained me as no challenge: I was so eager to fall, to be pulled down on hot ground, crushed fernsmell in my face and nauseous, blessedly nauseous again with the earth's slow spin.

They say there's no passion like a woman's for her child. Somebody, give me a little hope. Lie to me on this one.

To Practice the Thing

When I was very young, it was Concentration Camp. I used to like to play that in the bathtub especially. I'd pretend the tub was a cattle car, that it was carrying me to the camps and I was crammed in; that it was the last time I would see my mother and father and baby brother before we would arrive and be separated into the lines. I knew that children too small to work were killed immediately—I was six; that's the earliest I can remember playing it: the bathroom in the house on Johnson Avenue—so I knew I would be surely killed, that my brother would be killed and my parents too, eventually, miserable and starving in different barracks, not even able to comfort one another. I would crush myself up against the porcelain, trying to use as little space as possible, seeing bodies lapping around my feet and the baby crying, and then crying myself, imagining goodbye Mama, goodbye Papa, baby crushed under a guard's feet—

I would cry my eyes clean, it seemed. Everything would quiver and glow when I got out, the colors huge and shimmering, the love-feeling like a pain all through my chest and belly, and I would hurry to find all three of them, hugs and kisses, rocking Samuel, climbing into laps and doing chores unasked.

My mother told me only recently that it was always something of a family joke: how affectionate I was after a bath. They always wondered why, and advised the aunts of it as a tonic for their own children: "You should see the miracle a good bath works on Rachel!" What's hard to believe now is that I could have known and understood so much, so young; that they would have talked so freely in front of a six-year-old; that my mother, especially, who hated the topic, would have allowed it to be discussed in front of me. What morbidity must have enveloped our house! and yet it doesn't seem sad to me, merely what was.

Of course none of it had even touched us—I was six in 1970, after all. My parents and their parents before them had grown up in this country, middle and then upper-middle class. My mother's family intermarried all the time anyway, and left off most of the observances long ago. It only touched us through my father, through his imagination and through the imaginations of his men-friends who would sit up late in our living room and talk—angry, lugubrious, resigned—about horrors they'd only read and heard of.

But imagination is all that's really necessary, especially if it brings the vicarious thrill of the Terrible and the attendant preciousness of vision, as it did for me when I was a child, scripting out bathtub holocausts of my own. Much in the same way, saturated with romantic novels, I played Consumptive Heroine as an adolescent. (A redundant game, I realize now, since its drama hinges on the slow dance of decline we're all doing anyway. But you have to outgrow the vital throb and spring and sap of youth before that fully clicks home.)

Now it's quite succinct, the thing I do. Often when I'm driving alone—and I find it especially useful when Ben and I haven't been getting along well, and I'm on the way home and not particularly looking forward to pulling in the drive—I play Bouncing Betty. I spend a bit of time getting the details down (imagination again; I was still a child when Viet Nam was oozing and erupting): the heat, the murky dampness, wandering through a swamp exhausted but keen-sensed from fear, and then . . . the wrong step, the click, the awesome and horrific surety: to step off is to explode.

And I begin the summons, the calling, the bringing up of all the fragments, the faces, the music of voices, the perfect wild sweet melting fucks, every tiny moment—I make sure I'm on a fairly straight stretch for this part so I can concentrate; there's a workable bit of road after you turn off the loop—doing as closely as possible what I'd do in my mind if I were there, standing on that bastard, that soul-rapist of a bomb. Ben, of course; a couple of the lovers that preceded him; a clean view of my mother, singing over a flat of seedlings, her white hair slipping from its knot; my brother as a child and now in law school with his wife, plotting my nieces and nephews; a fight in the attic with Ben once, when I really *saw* him; walking alone up a mountain near Little Rock, singing the same song again and again until it sang me; the trances, the live prayers, the tomato well-sliced when the sun came through, the butcher block splashed with light . . . and then I drop my own little heart-bomb. Hannah, my own girl, my baby, my sweet thing waiting at home, still pudge-cheeked, still talking up a flock of poetry each time she tries to speak. My rose, my fox, my nerd. Like a slide projector on unstoppable fast-forward, the images of her, a thousand hers, swell and flicker and flash—and I step off. I step off. I kiss death, I welcome it into me like a hungry lover. I eat death in my mind. And then, because my heart still beats: a gasp, a sigh, a whole-body rush. The light and the freedom, the sear in the lungs. The jubilant scream of alive.

I have a minute or two then, before I turn left onto Albany. I wind down, breathe deeply, relax just enough to keep the poignant torn feeling in my chest intact. So that my house is vivid, sharp, its outlines clear and details clean when I pull up. The grass smells like grass, fresh and sweet under each crushing step, and my cry of gladness when I open the door, see her, see him, erupts without my cajoling.

It works, it works, it really does. All the la-di-da the poets give us about backward-spreading brightness, and death being the mother of beauty, and so on—it's all true, true, all my own sweet proven fact.

But there is a slight difficulty. As with any discipline, it can become routine. That's where imagination takes the stage; why I naturally, for instance, stopped imagining cattle cars when I'd grown to a certain age, and why tuberculosis and a bevy of other terminal illnesses gradually lost their charm. Even the Bouncing Betty exercise has lately begun to pall—not entirely, but the results aren't what they used to be. Sometimes I still feel a little faded, a little reluctant when I step up to the front porch. It bothers me a bit, because nothing new has suggested itself as a replacement.

Well, actually, one idea has been sort of toying with me, but I'm not sure. It's the shoes. It's his shoes that keep popping into my mind at odd moments when I'm daydreaming, or just lately even when I'm not. They were beautiful shoes, wingtips, very brown, very rich and glowing leather—I used to polish them myself when I was little—a deep glossy warm brown, a mahogany brown, with three little lace holes on either side of each tongue and soft thin brown cotton laces.

I keep imagining him looking down at them, the sight of the shoes filling his whole screen of vision as he began to summon and recall.

Or was he blank? Was it only a wild space for him, a wild space of tactile, visual, sensual imprints: only his mahogany shoes at the edge of the chair, only the green carpet, the floral sofa, the bay window and through it the backyard, our treehouse, and the faintly trafficked alley; the perpetual twinge in his left hip;

only the final sounds of a dog barking, a telephone ringing unanswered in the house next door? Or was all that invisible to him, intangible—as sometimes the actual road disappears when I drive the straight stretch, imagining? Was his vision filled with Mama, and did he ache and mourn and groan, guiltily knowing the wound he'd make in her that would not heal? Did he summon Sam, and feel a shredding in his gut? And did he imagine me? Did I flicker in front of his eyes like fluttering stabs of light, stabs of pain? Was I his rose, his angel, his moonflower, before he kicked the chair away?

Liking It Rough

I was not a wicked kid. Mischievous, yeah—or *mis-cheeev-yus*, as folks said it in any number of little East Texas towns where we lived. I liked to set the chickens free, to hide Pa's Tabasco sauce bottle behind other stuff in the icebox (which was bad because he used it nightly, shaking it over everything Ma cooked), to coax some kid's hesitating pony up the porch steps and into our front room.

Ma was a half-hearted whipper. She laughed too easy, and laughing took the strength out of her. Besides, I was her only child, her boy, her baby. "My Elvis," she would say, nuzzling my hair, her arms around me. "My king." If I could surprise her good, I wasn't likely to get beat. One time, when Ma was driving the pickup, the muffler and some pipe fell clean off. She pulled onto the dirt shoulder and went back and picked it up, threw it in the bed and stood there, leaning on the truck, laughing hard at a thing would piss most people off, maybe ruin their day. Pa could laugh, too, till his eyes were wet. They were good folks to have.

Once we moved to a town about as big as a spit-ring in the dust, just some one- and two-story buildings that clustered together at a crossroads and thinned out fast as the roads split and went their own ways. There was a post office, a feed store, a little grocery store with milk we bought often, tired vegetables, food in dusty cans, and comic books and candy. There were glass bottles of Grape Nehi, Coca-Cola, and root beer stacked on their sides in a silver-lidded cooler that hummed hot air at your feet. There was a barbershop and a couple of other buildings I can't recall because I never went into them.

But the most alluring part of this town, for a boy, anyway, was set back away from the buildings, up a little hill and a ways back into the pines, in a clearing you couldn't even see when you stood down on the feed store porch.

It was a genuine gallows from the olden days, with a drop you could work.

Well, on me and on the kids who'd always lived there, it exerted a powerful draw. Our folks didn't bother telling us to keep off it; there was no point. Might as well tell kids not to swim in a quarry. We'd run up the wooden stairs with objects in our hands—rocks, branches, someone's sister's doll—which we'd set on the drop and then, with a quick swish of the arm, let fall. We'd enact hangings with the slow ascent up the stairs, the blindfold, the noose knotted around each other's necks but the rope's free end dangling, which ruined the effect some but we weren't stupid.

It was fun and terrible to stand there in the blindfold, in the noose, the world black and all its sounds loud around you, some other kid saying our made-up semblance of last rites, and then waiting for the second—and they'd make you wait, too: the tight excited feeling in your stomach like when a tickling uncle suspends his hands just over your ribs and grins—and then you'd hear the wooden lever's clunk, and you'd fall through black space, hit the ground in a heap of banged bones. It gave me that carnival thrill. It was good to be the hanged man, and it was good to be the one who let him drop, making the condemned stand there tied, blind, nervous excitement quivering his mouth corners. I could see why the grownups had liked it.

Sometimes we lay under the ground beneath it for its good shade, there in the sparse grass, talking, telling what jokes we knew over and over, making them better with changes and tweaks until they were our own jokes, jokes by kid-committee, and we'd laugh ourselves hysterical. Sometimes we'd smell the dirt to see if we could smell where the come had gone, but all the dirt smelled the same and we figured either the come had stayed in the pants or it had all been way too long ago. From a distance we must have looked crazy, a pack of boys crawling on our bellies, sniffing at tufts of grass.

I never got up to mischief to be cruel. We'd lived in a lot of farm towns, and I'd seen cruel. I've seen kids play basketball with newborn kittens, smack them off the backboards of their graying barns and let them fall through a stringless hoop to the dirt. I've seen them wedge knife tips under the edge of a caught fish's eyeball and gouge it out while the thing was still flopping. I've seen them tie their little brothers to a handmade cross and leave them in the backyard to cry and yell all afternoon while we went elsewhere, or chop a snake to bits, working from the tail forward so it felt it, as they said, till the last possible minute, its small desperate eye like a black jewel.

I was not, my mama said, that kind of kid. I liked folks, and I liked animals, liked to just watch them do their different animal things, and I liked to laugh with my parents. Little kids always made me feel like helping them, reading to them or showing them how to do something. I wasn't like the ones who used their daddies' lighters to melt the cats' whiskers so they'd walk funny like drunks. But I watched; I didn't interfere. I just observed, like watching just another kind of animal at its ways. To avoid being the target of an experiment, I followed simple rules. Hang out with kids my own size or smaller. Be good to everybody, so if things go bad, no one sees it as a chance to get back at you. You don't want to be at the mercy of more than one.

I didn't think of the kitten-killers as bullies, though I'd heard the word. They were just kids, crueler but of the same species. Even though we moved a lot, there were ways you could tell who was likely to be a kitten-killer: if he was more gaunt than the other kids—but not always; sometimes the skinniest, poorest ones were sweet and meek. If his daddy was known to be a drunk or brawler. If his ma slapped or yelled at him in public. If he smelled of urine and his hair stuck up in unwashed twigs all over his head. Or if his sister was mean. That was a guarantee: if you met a mean girl, it was a surefire thing her brothers were meaner.

My pa had a rifle, like most folks, but he had a Colt .45 as well. He'd lived in Dallas after the army—and before he'd met the prettiest, sweetest girl on God's green Earth, as he said—and Dallas folks were none too kind to a country boy. Hence the .45. He kept it under his side of the bed. He'd shown me how to clean it a couple times, but the rifle was the only gun I'd fired.

We'd been living outside the gallows town in a little rented house—we were there for harvest, Pa said, and if we liked it, we'd stay—for only a couple of weeks when I began to draw the curiosity of one Tanner Keady. Tall, bony, with black hair cropped so close to his bullet-head it looked more like a shadow, and pale blue eyes, and arm muscles like walnuts rippling against ropes, he did not stink like urine, but there was a smell that came off him, a smell of something hot and bitter—maybe just his sweat, since he was older, fourteen, starting to get grown. I was ten. I laughed a lot, made friends fast, could fish and drive a tractor and do a perfect swan dive off the bluff above the river, and I had that shine on me of affection and plenty of food, that shine that drove some bullies nuts. Because of an operation my ma'd had and sometimes cried about, I was an only child and guaranteed to stay one, which was a rare thing to be in East Texas, and everyone said my ma was a tender woman and my father a good man. In church I sat between them and my father's arm rested on the pew behind me, and they'd smile at each other when the preacher talked on love.

It was natural for someone like Tanner to hate me.

It started in the feed store. It was blistering hot and bright outside, and my hands were plunged wrist-deep in a barrel of cool nails in the shady bowels of the store, when suddenly he was there, too close, standing right in next to me like he was going to kiss me or something.

"You ain't from around here," he said, leaning in, taller than me.

It sounded like something in a cowboy movie. I made the mistake of laughing.

He put his hand between my shoulders, shoved my own hands deeper in the nails, and held me there.

"Something funny?"

There were no grownups close by. If I hollered, Tanner would slither away long before Mr. Hollifield got back to our corner of the store. I could just answer no, play humble. And so I did. But giving in, I could tell, wouldn't make him go away. He'd just get his appetite whetted for more.

But the thing about a bully: he's always already picked on a bunch of other kids, so he's got a whole lot of ill will going against him. While nobody's going to take him on alone, there's strength in numbers, and all they want is someone who's willing to go first.

The biggest twelve-year-old in town was called Flounder, and he was packed with meat and muscle and a little soft belly he liked to feed, and my ma would hand us generous plates through the back door of the diner where she worked, and we'd sit on the steps and eat and talk. He liked to hear about other places I'd lived. He'd been to the county seat once but couldn't remember it. He was my best friend there, I guess you could say, and there were other boys that sometimes hung around with us.

In adulthood I have met people who knew and played with girls as children, and women who claim to have played with boys, but in the East Texas towns where I grew up, the girls were another tribe, conducting their business on the same soil but having no dealings with us. It's true that if you liked a particular girl, she would then become visible and meaningful for the duration of your interest. Otherwise and as a mass, they were irrelevant. But if you looked, you could see them.

Tanner Keady had a sister, Liz Ann, and she was not mean. She was his little sister, about eight, and she walked around like a sleeping person, placid. She'd obey anything a grownup or older kid told her to do. She made no trouble and no noise. She was skinny and wore her dresses old and her black hair in two sharp pigtails, and I don't know if her eyes were blue like Tanner's or not because they were mostly on the ground. She worked hard to be invisible and pretty much succeeded. You could see where she would have been a pretty girl, too, if she'd plumped up a little and learned to smile, so it was a shame.

Little kids, like I said, always made me want to be nice to them, and one day Liz Ann walked alone past the back of the diner when me and Flounder were sitting back there talking, over our second lunches of the day.

"Hey," I called to her, but she kept her head down and walked faster, her shoulders curling in. "Hey, you want some tomato?" She slowed, stopped, and turned toward us, looked us over as though looking for a trap. Fact is, I hate tomato. "For real," I said, "you can have it," holding up the two slices I'd taken off my sandwich. She came closer, and Flounder smiled at me. He opened his own sandwich and pulled out the cheese. It was easy after that, like coaxing a cat out from under a barn. She sat down and ate the tomatoes, Flounder's cheese, and all four of our slices of bread, and then we let her scoop the mayonnaise blobs off our plates with her finger. She stared at us, eyes wide, her finger popped in her mouth like a baby, and didn't interrupt while we talked about stuff. After that she came by every day, and sometimes I'd tell stories my pa had read me, just this and that, Arabian Nights and Goldilocks and suchlike. Flounder liked to hear them, too. But that was the only time we'd see her, and when we got up to go play at the gallows or swim or go fishing, she went her own way.

One day the three of us were there, Liz Ann perched on the bottom stair eating peach slices from the plate my ma had made up just for her, looking up and smiling as I told Little Red Riding Hood. I was at the part when she opens the door and sees the wolf in her grandma's bed, when Tanner Keady rounded the corner. He wasn't a whistler, and he walked with a quiet tread, so we didn't see him until he was almost upon us, and he came on us loud.

"Liz Ann Keady, what the hell you doing?" He grabbed her by the hair and yanked her up. The plate fell and cracked into two white half-ovals, the food scattering everywhere on the steps and in the dirt. "You gonna pay for that, now? Are you? Look what you done," he yelled, and then they were moving fast away from us, him dragging her, her feet scrambling to keep her upright. "You stay away from my sister," he yelled, "or I'll kill you. I'll goddamn kill you both."

Flounder and I were still sitting, shocked, our plates on our knees, our hands frozen in position where they'd been when he appeared. Liz Ann didn't even try to glance our way, just got herself hauled and yelled out of sight. We looked at each other then, and I picked up the food and put it on the stacked halves of the plate. I wasn't worried. "Aw, shit," my ma would say and laugh with her hands on her hips. "There goes part of my pay." And she'd ruffle my hair and tell me to get on out of there. I'd never been yanked to my feet like that in my life, and my hand crept up and pulled my hair, hard, to see how it felt.

"You think she's going to get into trouble at home, too? With her folks?" Flounder asked. It hadn't occurred to me, but she had been eating secret food from the diner. Maybe she wasn't allowed.

"I don't know. Maybe."

"Maybe we ought to go out there to her house and see," he said.

"You're crazy." Getting between some girl and her daddy's belt was nothing I wanted to do.

"But he might tell them she stole it," Flounder said, scratching his scabbed and pillowy brown knee. "You could tell them your ma gave it to her." He had a point.

"I don't know."

"But Jakey," he said in a low voice, not looking at me, "she's so little."

I sighed and stood up.

"Okay."

Flounder knew where the Keadys lived, a long way out a dirt road. The trees thinned out and disappeared, and it was just fields and pastureland and scrub. The day was fever-bright, and I wished we were swimming instead. The Keadys had about six kids and their own farm, and we could see as we got close that their horses and cows weren't any more filled out than Tanner and Liz Ann. The livestock lifted their heads dully to stare at us as we passed. Close to the unpainted wood house, there were chickens wandering around, and about a dozen wooden outbuildings with their metal roofs rusted orange, with pieces of farm equipment, balers and so on, rusted and lying on their sides. Rusted lengths of chicken wire, barbed wire, lay twisted in the grass like sculpture. It looked like a lot of farms, but there was something eerie about it. It was hot and quiet and eye-squintingly bright, with just the hot rise and fall of cicadas as the only waves of sound. I didn't hear anyone yelling, or anyone crying, or the sound of a belt.

"It's all right. Let's go," I said.

"Wait." Flounder held up a hand, and then I heard it, faintly: the splash of water and a muttering voice. Without warning, my heavy, slow, good-natured buddy suddenly fell into a crouch like some army guy doing reconnaissance, then started running fast toward an outbuilding. Ten yards from me, he paused and looked back to where I still stood, astonished. He shrugged, like *What the hell are you waiting for?* and crooked his hand impatiently at me, waving me over. As if loosed from the soil by his certainty, my feet moved fast in his path. When we got to the building, he slowed, put a finger on his lips, and sidled up next to it. We listened, panting as silently as we could in the heat.

"On three," Flounder mouthed, holding up three fingers, but then he picked up a rock, and I picked up one, too, and he nodded. We could hear Tanner's bitter voice as Flounder's fingers slowly folded down.

"You go near them boys again, I'll kill you." There was a splash, and then silence, and then a splash again and a gasp, a girl's gasp. "You hear me? I'll fucking kill you."

On three, we looked together, me crouched behind Flounder, and what I saw has never left me. Tanner's back was to us, and he stood with his sister next to a homemade watering trough, which was just half a steel drum propped on concrete blocks

27

to catch the rain. The fingers of one hand were twined through her hair, and as we watched he forced her head down in the water again. But what clutched my vision and my gut was that her cotton dress was hiked up around her waist, and his other hand was dug inside her gray underpants, twisting and working.

"You hear me?" he muttered at her underwater head. Her bare legs shook.

"Jesus," breathed Flounder, and then his rock was flying before I saw him move his arm, and I threw mine, and then Tanner was screaming, clutching at his face, and Liz Ann was scrambling away, and then he had turned and seen us and was moving toward us, wet blood coming from between his fingers down his neck, and we knew how fast and light he was so we didn't look back until we were in the road, but then he was nowhere.

"Keep going," I panted, but Flounder said to wait, so we hung there in the road for long seconds until we saw him reappear on the porch of the house with a shotgun cradled in his arms, and we spun and did not stop running as we heard the reports in the hot still air, once, twice, three times as we ran farther and farther away.

Tanner had made a lot of enemies in the twelve-and-under crowd, and some of them had their puberty upon them and were no longer small. And with Flounder's newly revealed skills at my side, I was ready to think of a plan. Something in my stomach had gone sick when we'd looked around that corner, the sick of a kitten hitting barn wood. I knew that girl. She was a nice girl. She had looked up at us while we told stories, and she'd eaten her food and said thank you all quiet and sweet. I wanted to kill Tanner. And there was more to it, too, something other than the sick stomach or the anger, something I couldn't put a name to, something about the rusted-out machines and her little thin legs trembling, and the hot still air and no parents being home to stop it. Something forlorn, something about the green scum on the surface of the stagnant water and the line it left on her jaw and temple when he pulled her head out. I'd worn old graying underwear most of my life, sometimes even with holes in it. But somehow it was worse on a girl.

The plan was easy. It relied on Tanner's own weakness, his desire to take from someone littler. We got Angel to be the bait.

Angel's real name was Tommy, and he was eleven, but he looked eight, with big blue eyes and blond curling hair and an innocent smile that no one who knew him believed. Lucky for us, Tanner didn't know him except to beat him up.

It would be Angel's job to walk through the crossing roads of our town with a brand-new beautiful watch, which was actually my father's good watch that had been his father's, which I was borrowing for the occasion from its nest in his sock drawer. It was Angel's job to show it to all and sundry and talk about how much he loved his beautiful new pocketwatch his grandma had sent him from Lake Charles, and then to say how he was going to spend the whole afternoon in the pines alone, watching squirrels and timing them with the second hand. And then once he had announced it, he was to wander slowly, slowly up the hillside path, la-di-da, past the gallows, chasing a butterfly or two, and on into the woods. From our hiding places, we watched him as he wound aimlessly across the grass. It wasn't ten minutes before Tanner Keady loped up the hill, grinning his purposeful leer. From our various lookouts, we watched him enter the dark shade of the pines, and we moved in.

We knew that as soon as Angel hit cover, he'd start to run, and he'd run until he came to the first big clearing, so we headed there and fanned out silently around it, crouching in position. He played it beautifully, stretched out on his belly in the pine needles, humming, my father's watch a full arm's length away on the ground, gleaming in what little sunlight made it down to the forest floor. When Tanner found him, he looked up and smiled his cherubic smile.

"Hi, Tanner," he chirped. "Whatcha doing?" And as Tanner snarled and bent for the watch, the intrepid Flounder slid up with his silent army tactics and bashed a block of wood into the base of Tanner's skull. Tanner dropped to the cushion of pine needles, and thirteen boys of varying ages emerged from the shadows, our eyes alight.

When Tanner Keady finally came to, he could not move. He was on his knees, his ankles bound with rope and his wrists tied behind him, and he had, from where he knelt on the gallows platform, a beautiful view of our town and, in the distance, the river. We had him on his knees so we'd seem taller and he'd be confused. Only six of us were there, which is as many Ku Klux Klan hoods and robes as we'd been able to rustle up from the high back shelves of our houses, where they lay folded with shame or secret pride. Though it felt bad to use them, we knew they'd be scary. The rest watched from the woods. Flounder was there under his hood, and me, and four other guys Tanner had personally tormented. We all used deep voices when we talked.

"Tanner Keady, do you know why you are here?" I asked. The preacher's son murmured stuff about Heaven and Hell and eternal rest; we thought it would be a good effect. "Tanner Keady, do you know why you are here?" I said again, trying to sound ominous, like the Ghost of Christmas Past. He shook his head; we'd taped his mouth. "You are here at the behest of the Tribe of Justice. In the matter of hurting Liz Ann Keady and beating up the kids of this town, you are hereby judged guilty."

"Guilty," echoed the five kids around me.

"Guilty!" came cries from the trees. Tanner's head jerked around, his eyes wild and scared.

Coup de grace is a phrase I'd learned from the books my pa read aloud about swordfighters and pirates and musketeers. I pulled ours out, the black gleaming Colt .45, and Tanner's eyes grew huger than I'd ever seen human eyes get. The pupils got so big that the blue almost disappeared for a second, and then he looked up at me, making anxious pleading sounds through the tape.

Those sounds froze me. I felt sick suddenly, seeing him like that, knowing I was doing it, feeling my own face in the hood. I couldn't, for a minute, go on, and my throat swelled, and I thought I was going to cry. I hadn't reckoned I'd go soft. I understood all of a sudden why executioners wore a hood, even when the person to be killed was definitely bad. I couldn't do it, and my hand with the Colt fell to my side. Tanner's wide eyes narrowed again, and as Flounder's familiar brown hand reached out toward the gun, I saw in them a flicker of triumph, that he knew as clear as if we'd been standing there regular that we were all just a bunch of little kids, and he'd get each of us alone and make us pay and pay. The kind of person Tanner Keady was, if you were going to let him live, you had to scare him bad. I pulled my hand away from Flounder's.

"And the wages of sin," I said, "is death." I rubbed the muzzle familiarly around his cheek, like a friendly nuzzling cat, and his eyes widened again, and I could see droplets spring out on his forehead that were not just from the heat. I put the end of it in his ear, then at his temple. "You'll never hurt anyone again." I cocked it. Tears rolled from his eyes, and terrible sounds came through the tape, but I saw like a photograph the picture of him shoving his sister's head down and the bunching sick movement under the gray cloth. "Goodbye, Tanner," I whispered, and I pulled the trigger. A quiet metallic click sounded in the air.

"Aw, shit," I said, as planned. Tanner had slumped over on his side at the sound of the gun not firing. He was trembling, and his eyelids were fluttering a bit. I felt a sad surge of pity again.

But Flounder, who'd suffered at his hands for years, had none of my qualms.

"Well, boys," he said in a low, tough voice, like he was talking to a posse, "I guess we're just gonna have to hang him."

Tanner shook his head wildly back and forth, moaning, and I felt sick again. The other boys fastened the noose around his neck and demonstrated how attached it was. They tied the blindfold on. They made quite a production of saying how the rope was attached right well to the scaffold, though of course they undid it. Flounder tore the tape from Tanner's mouth.

"Any last words?"

"Please," the boy said, his voice a cracked whisper, and he was just a boy then, helpless and frightened and blind. Someone pulled the lever, and we let him drop.

It was a long fall, but we'd all fallen it ourselves. We waited to see that he was moving and that there was no blood, and then we hightailed it into the trees, stripping off our ancestral gear and running gleefully to the river, where we swam and jumped off the highest rocks without hesitation, feeling invincible. In the evening, we went back to the deserted gallows and told and retold it in glorious detail.

By nightfall the robes and hoods and watch and Colt had all been stored away, and Tanner Keady had been spotted hobbling homeward. He was a shadowy presence after that. He left us alone.

It's a good thing for a boy to feel: like he's come to town and made a difference. One autumn evening, Pa announced that we'd be moving on.

I've been a cop in Houston for a lot of years now, enough years to know that what we did didn't save Liz Ann. I've seen the broken people, and they don't fix easy. At ten, I couldn't know that. At forty, I leave that part of the work to gentler folks.

But we did stop Tanner Keady from hurting again, from hurting anyone else, and I'll admit I did acquire a taste for it, what they call rough justice, and let's just say there have been things I've done. Stuff I've seen on calls has made me cry afterwards, and stuff my buddies and I have done has sometimes avenged my outraged sense of justice and sometimes made me laugh until my eyes were wet and sometimes both.

But I swear I've never in my life laughed as hard as I did lying under that gallows in the dusk with my friends, rolling in the grass, the bitter, satisfying stench of where we'd scared Tanner Keady pissless still rising from the dusty earth.

Musing

No one here needs to know why I shoved a Papermate Flexgrip Ultrafine pen into my palm until its plastic casing snapped and blue ink ran in streams with my blood. They don't need to know why. They just need to clean me up, give me my tetanus shot, and send me home.

When I was a nubile undergrad, dressed in leggings and Goodwill hoodies, my writing professor was already old. He had a gray cloud of a beard tinged with ginger and a bald head. He wore frail-looking silver-rimmed glasses and the estimable paunch of late middle age and a wife on his arm at all the faculty events, and she was just the sort of wife some academics have. She looked practically academic herself, with a gray cloud of hair to match her husband's beard, and she wore those close-toed Birkenstocks they wear, in some colorless color like taupe, and knee socks, and nondescript skirts or pants—but always (over the black turtleneck) a vest or little jacket hand-woven in Ecuador or Guatemala, with threads of purple and turquoise mixed in among the black and white. Her earrings were always very interesting and busy and ethnic. She was that woman, and the faint aroma of mothballs clung to her, wafting as a bottom note under the nice lily perfume, and she came in on my writing professor's arm but would soon release it in favor of a clear plastic cup of white wine and a little plate of whatever was on the table, and she would rove the room separately from her husband because after all they'd been at the university so long now she knew everyone practically as well as he did and could effortlessly pick up threads of conversations abandoned at the last party or reading or lecture and carry right on. She was an entirely self-sufficient mingler, and the ginger-tinged beard of my professor would wag among little knots of people that did not include her, and they rarely seemed even to notice one another as the hour or two wore on until at last, at an appropriate moment of dwindling festivity, they would suddenly, as if by some mysterious marital radar, appear at one another's sides, murmur their thanks to the host, and relink their comfortable arms. Out they would amble, as calmly as if scripted or paid for, a marvel of conjugal amicability, and I suppose it was inevitable that at some point my scheming and contriving little mind would take it upon itself to wonder if that very certitude, that connubial echolocation system, in its predictable placidity, wasn't somehow implicated in my professor's flushed encouragement of my work, in his effusive assessments of my plotless first-person short-shorts about brutish sex against dumpsters or in study carrels as being so very promising. He was generous. "I'd like to see more like this," he'd say, shuffling and stroking my pages during our one-on-one conferences in his little office with the door half closed and nobody really around, since he had to schedule our meetings after his late-afternoon classes because his schedule was so demanding. "Develop further," the margins would say when I got my manuscripts back. "Ground this in sensory detail," and "Specificity!"

It was always twilight in the hall when I went to see him, hopeful about my talent and the possibilities he might open up for me, and his small window would deepen its blue and then go black as he talked. He could talk for a tremendously long time. He had a fine voice and knew a lot of words, and his tone would develop a fondness once he'd been going for a while, as if he were gently blessing each syllable as it left his lips—as if he were doing it a kindness, really, by sending it into the world. Sometimes my legs would get restless, just sitting there listening, and I'd have to fold and unfold them, fold and unfold, fold and unfold while his voice droned on, and his voice would go droning on and I felt as though in a trance, and his eyes would watch my legs fold and unfold as though hypnotized by the smooth black lengths of them encased in their 90 percent cotton, 10 percent spandex leggings, and sometimes I'd stare down at them, too, and run my hands down the smooth lengths of them and stretch a little and feel like I was underwater or asleep or dead in a dream. Finally he would finish by urging me to read this book or that book I would never read, and I'd agree to do so and thank him very much for his time and encouragement, and he'd say, "My pleasure. My pleasure," and I'd leave and all along the dark sidewalk to the parking lot I'd glance up and his light would still be on, and when I drove off his light would still be on, and sometimes when I drove by again quite late for some reason or no reason, still it would be on.

A very few years later, which is to say last week, he called to say he'd gotten most of the stories in his recent collection that way: those nights after I'd left, in the strange elated silence, as he put it, that I'd leave him in. The collection was nominated for the National Book Award, but then a lot of things are, and he wanted to thank me, and so he thanked me, and he apologized for not having thanked me in the acknowledgments.

"Not at all," I said, a response I thought pleasingly open to alternative readings.

Now I walk to the parking lot in the dark, my bandaged hand

like a thick white mitten, a paw, a puddle of tape, and the tetanus shot medicine still spreads and burns in my flesh. I'll have to drive with my left.

It was confusing, being a muse, and now at twenty-six I should know better than to be shoving pens into my hand but am left still wondering if my talent lay at all in the writing, or merely in the folding and unfolding of my black-clad legs, the way I ran my fingers through the soft long strands of my dark hair, stroked and tugged the silver hoops in my ears as dusk fell and his talk lowered us gently into our shared crepuscular trance—or if it actually lay in the brutish sex I had in study carrels and the bathrooms of dance halls and in alleys, bent forward with my hands braced against a reeking dumpster, my throat clogging with the rot-smell as I came, just another kind of stabbing, another kind of wound I did to myself with what I could find.

Independence Day

An agave can be many things, its tough gray-green spikes frozen in their waving like the stilled arms of an anemone in the desert's long-parched sea. The bison of the Aztecs, the agave proffers its lathering innards as soap; its vicious brown-pointed tips to men as arrowheads or to women as threaded needles ready-made (with a strand of fibers left attached); its deep rubbery layers as condoms; its thinner dry sheets near the surface as paper; its fibers as the thread for weaving, tough but softening with washing and time. If a flowering plant has been cultivated nearby, its blossoms can be used to rub hot pink or tomato red into the agave's pale fibers just as they're stripped from the plant. And don't forget mezcal, the intoxication buried at the agave's base, the root of our tequila.

Yes: the agave gives us love and frenzy, the soap to clean up afterwards and the clothes to put back on, and the codices to record our acts and visions. A whole culture can be read in the pith of the agave, if one knows how to read: a testament to the resourcefulness of a people and to the generosity of the gods we used to love, who scattered such bounty over the dry land.

Yet when the white men came, they saw only a forbidding weed, a thorned sentry tall as a man.

In the year of our Christ 1848, I was some two decades into my life, minding my business and flirting with one José Maria

Loiaza—*a quiet, inoffensive sort of man*, the papers called him later—just living quietly, when somebody somewhere signed something, and suddenly the town of San Jose, where I'd lived since my parents moved us north from Jalisco, was no longer home. Los estados unidos ahora. México no more. When José asked me to marry him, we headed farther north, and east into the mountains, for freedom. Raised on haciendas to know our place, we worked in wood, José and me, him a carpenter and rough carver, and me learning with sharp-tipped tools how to hew the fine detail. We thought maybe there would be call for us in the little villages, and we would find peace: the crisp light of mountain mornings, the scent of pinesap and cold streams. Birdsong.

But then somebody somewhere found some gold, and suddenly people—men, white men—were flooding everywhere, craving that useless shine. Quick and dirty riches. They came alone or in little bands through the mountains, risking death, these men without women or soap. They staggered along the streets of Downieville, loving nothing more than whiskey, cards, and fast wealth.

Frederick Cannon, rushing in your rush for gold, did my gold shoulders disarray your mind? I was one of Downieville's few women. And brown. Did you think to pan beneath my skirt that day you ripped our door from its leather hinges, reveling in fresh statehood, stumbling with your friends down Main Street, a celibate and frustrated brotherhood of miners-forty-niners, your fingers sunk all day in the earth's wetness, sifting for a treasure you could sell?

July 4, 1851. God Bless Your America, los estados unidos ahora, when a mere three years ago it had been home and mine. Praise God and liberty. Your revelries went on all day, guns fired into the air, bright bunting strung around the general store, whiskey downed in gulps, your faces painted red and white, chickens and hogs massacred for your culinary delight. Your feast of grease. When you and your drunken miner friends wove down Main Street, shouting your national pride, loud, fueled by your clogged cocks, did the closed door of our little house offend you? Did it confuse you, there in the mountains, in the place you'd come for your fortune of last resort—where you'd expected that everything, finally, would open to you? Were its shut boards the final straw after months of your invisibility to me? How goddamn pissed off you'd been when I wouldn't notice you, the tension so hot and thick I could smell its stench when I went to draw water from the Yuba. When I lifted the clay jar to my head, your gaze sifted my dress like fingers.

That evening, July 4th, when José came home, our wooden door lay in the street. Main Street, USA. Without shame you did it, Frederick Cannon, knocked my door from its frame, threw it down, and came with your stink into the place that was mine. Your friends, drunk on America and whiskey and our mezcal, waited laughing in the road.

You left with my shawl, its cobalt tassels swinging in the hot evening wind.

Plenty of women can handle a blade, and I was a carver, a worker in sharp detail. When you stumbled past the next morning, groaning with tequila suffering, José stopped you, demanding payment for the door's repair. (The broken door. That's what he said. Some things cannot be spoken.) You spat in the dust, called my husband a bad name.

"Well, hello, my dear," you said when I materialized in the empty frame, your breath thicker, stale and rotten, "and how are you today?" You swept low with your crumpled hat in hand, a mocking bow.

I only stared. Your eyes got ugly then. The light was the high bright light of morning, and it was my pleasure to watch you squint. I called you pig and wished you all the pain mezcal could bring.

And then you called me *whore*. The easy, open door.

I heard the sound of thumping footsteps in my ears. It was my blood. The wide world grew quiet. Even the hot breeze hushed.

"What did you name me?"

You said it again, the sweat-stink rising off you.

"Would you dare to name me that in my own house?" I asked, withdrawing under the shadowing shelter of our roof. I'd helped to hoist the beams onto the joists myself. Inside I stood poised upon a brink: if you left, you left.

But you followed like the bellowing fool you were, crossing the threshold we'd made with our hands—

Well, I shoved my Bowie blade inside you, and you died. Slowly, coughing blood and hatred, the shock alive at last in your eyes.

My husband cried, "Josefa! My God, what have you done?"

So many miles I have already come, from Jalisco and the pueblo of my ancestors in Atotonilco el Alto, to San Jose with my parents, and at last to this stupid mountain town where we'd thought to make our wedded home, this fraternity of pigs, where we tried one year to live in happiness, thinking we could ignore what lay around us, thinking we could build with our hands all we'd need. Foolishly trusting that a closed door promised safety. Hundreds of miles have I come to this place, crossing deserts, mountains, fording fast rivers in rainy weather, granting wide berths to snakes and wolves.

To walk now onto this bridge over the blue Yuba is easy for me. The boards of the makeshift platform are rough, left unplaned in the excitement of the men. No great distance, this little drop.

In Sacramento once, I met the loveliness of roses and breathed their lifting scent, but John Rose, the white rancher pressed into emergency service as Judge Lynch, is nothing like them. Not flower or song, the makeshift Judge Rose ladled down his strict justice, as brutal and efficient as he's rumored to be with his Mexican ranch-hands: my trial the same day, a verdict and sentence in minutes. Then came the lengthy public justification as the newspapermen busily scribbled their accounts. Judge Rose's words went on and on: a woman killing miners, stabbing citizens? A nation must not abide such a bringer of fear into their civilized midst, and so on. And more: I was unwomanly, unnatural, a female wielding weapons, my brown face unreadable and thus forever dangerous ... The crowd lapped up the rousing sounds as his speech spun reasonable excuses for my death.

So this is the Yankee justice.

They ask for my last words. Suddenly the flute of my mother's voice comes back to me, a little song she used to sing on melancholy afternoons: *Nobody, nobody, nobody, truly lives on earth.* Now I was learning its truth in my flesh. Now I was going to the place of defleshing. The scent of copal smoke seemed to fill my nostrils, and I knew what words to leave.

"I would do the same again if I was so provoked." I let my voice float out over the sweating faces of men red with rage—drunk men who had made no success in the regular white world of the East and so came here, tough and hungry with quick greed, the beads of fat from yesterday's feast still lacing their jowls. Their united states of yelling. My good voice floating above them, my speech clearer than any mission bells.

My name is Josefa Juvera Loaiza. Let it be known and remembered. My date of birth: unknown. My devotion to my quiet

42

man: complete. My age at death: twenty-six or so, said witnesses. Some said twenty-three. The only woman ever hanged in California, newly of the USA, newly a state. A girl who walked always with a cross at my throat, who loved only La Virgen, mi familia, my husband, the land and wind and the tools of my hands. A woman whose only crime was to say, *No, some things are not for you to take.*

I throw my hat to the ground, unpin my black braids for the noose, and step up onto the makeshift stage.

The Yuba ripples below, its silk the same blue as my stolen shawl, the rage inside me so calm. To fall through this hot, dusty air into heaven is no fall at all.

A Time of Snow

I came of age in a time of snow. Chains wrapped my tires. My arms were lean from shoveling. I started work at dawn and left town each afternoon at five, so my days seemed like an endless string of laboring hours that opened and closed with slow, cautious driving through darkness, the road a carved tunnel through snow, my hands tense on the wheel for well over an hour each way between Halford and the reservation. It got so at night my hands would cramp, and I had to soak them in hot water like an old woman.

It was then, in that exhausted winter of my twenty-second year, that I learned the secret of rich people.

I'd been cleaning with my mom since I was twelve. She had a reputation for never stealing, not even a spoon, and the housewives of Halford, North Dakota, trusted me because of that. I'd gotten my own houses and my own used car when I was seventeen. I worked hard and knew what spotless was. I asked few questions. I barely spoke to the men, and I wore shapeless shirts and no makeup, so I made the middle-aged women who hired me feel safe. I wore my black hair back and braided. At twenty-two, I had ten nice houses near the campus. Doing two a day, I had the weekends off, and I made more than most of the men on my road at home.

At twenty-two I thought of marriage, not college, but working near the campus made me wonder. Some of the women I worked for, their husbands taught at the university or were vice-presidents there, and their children went there free or flew out east if they were smart. *Out east.* That's all the women ever said about it, but you could tell they were proud. Talking to their friends, that is, or on the phone. They didn't waste it on me.

I'd kept my legs shut like my mother scolded me, so I had no kids, which was unusual for my age. With my earnings and my body and no drinking and what people said was the good head on my shoulders, I was a fine catch, but I didn't feel like getting caught. It was hard, because I thought about sex a lot, every day, till it nearly drove me crazy and every busted-down man on the reservation looked good, but I just kept working and taking my money to First National and wondering what I'd do next.

My mom and daddy wanted me settled close enough to see my chimney's smoke and then some grandkids. I wasn't sure.

Cleaning houses had complicated things. The houses I cleaned had framed photographs of canyons and mountains and beaches, so different from North Dakota. Cities all lit up at night, twinkling. And just about every house I cleaned had a print hanging somewhere of a pointed metal building, and one of the ladies said, "Why, that's the Eiffel Tower, dear," with her hand to her throat when I asked. So I had the sense of things being kept from me.

I knew my money could be put down on a little frame house down the road from my family's, a house for me and my pick of the reservation men. Or it could take me far away from Fort Franklin and Halford and anything I'd ever known. I was wavering.

No one knew this.

I'd started cleaning the Hewitts' house three years earlier, when their daughter Miss Julia had been a senior at Halford High.

She graduated and went away to college. Now she was home for Christmas, back from out east.

I was not romantic about Christmas. To me, it just meant more little things to dust. It meant pretending to be all excited about other people's fancy stuff and presents, then going home to cold board floors at night.

Miss Julia Hewitt had no problems. Her father was some big muckety-muck at the university. His office at home was hung with photographs of golf courses around the world where he had personally golfed. It had a wide desk, and the leather sofa was often made up for sleeping, about which I was shrewd enough to make no comment. He had broad shoulders and a face like Gregory Peck. Mrs. Hewitt gave parties and got her hair done twice a month. Young Miss Julia had long smooth hair, gold and shining like cornsilk, that fell in smooth ripples down her back like a bolt of cloth. Her eyes were far apart and blue, with curved eyebrows plucked thin as a baby's, and she had a baby's little pink bud-mouth. She had a bedroom with wall-to-wall carpeting and matching cherry-wood furniture, a bookcase full of books, a gold-framed mirror rimmed with paper flowers and ticket stubs, and her own clean bathroom. While Miss Julia was away, Mrs. Hewitt kept both rooms all closed up like a temple, waiting. Once a week, I ran a cloth over the nearly dustless surfaces.

And now Miss Julia was back, poised on sofas and chairs with her back straight and her ankles crossed, her knees together inside their pale wool skirts and her strand of pearls draped neatly over a cashmere sweater. She had stacks of them in different colors on a shelf in her closet.

When I saw her perched like an ornament on the edge of a chair, it was hard not to think of the nails driven in the wall over my bed, how my clothes hung near enough to touch at night, how turning eighteen had earned me only the old sheet that separated me from my parents and brothers and sisters and let me privately ease the hunger that rode me. How at home we ate in shifts at the table because there were only four chairs and my mom wanted us to grow up with manners, not scattered all over creation with our plates in our hands. The Hewitts' table had six chairs around it and two leaves tucked in the pantry, and I laid it for two—now three—on the days I cleaned. Placemats. Two forks on the left, a knife on the right, a fork and spoon head to foot above the plate. A glass for water and one for wine. Matching cloth napkins rolled in rings of mother-of-pearl.

I did not dislike Julia Hewitt. She seemed a creature of another order. Her job in the world—as I knew from her senior year—was to talk on the phone about dances and curl in the window-seat reading, while mine was to move silently about the house, cleaning up the dust that was made up of tiny particles that flew off the bodies of the Hewitts and landed in a gray coating on their glossy furniture, and scrubbing the crusted particles of food that clung to their dishes and forks, and vacuuming up the crud that crumbled from the soles of their glossy shoes, and sponging from the porcelain of their toilets the tiny brown and yellow and red particles that came out of the Hewitts' bodies and were not flushed away. And so on. If you were going to make a living cleaning houses, you put away your desire for forks stamped sterling and soft pretty clothes. You kept your mouth and mind snapped shut, refusing to taste any of it or even speak of it.

But when Julia came home from out east this time, she was different. The compact we'd once had, she broke. No longer did I walk unnoticed past her. I was there. I was even, in my way, a person. She'd decided that.

"Do you know who Sylvia Plath is?" she asked one day, holding a book open in one hand.

"No, miss." I kept dusting. We called them *miss* then.

"Listen," she said, and she read a poem to me. Sometime about halfway through, my hand with its rag stopped moving, and I turned to watch her read. She paced up and down the living room, clutching the book with both hands. When she stopped, she looked up at me with shining eyes, as if waiting for me to clap, or cheer, or talk back to her in that same strange language of the book. I didn't know what to say. What she'd read felt hot and angry, with sex in it. Hunger.

"Well?" she said. Her voice pushed at me. Her eyes looked fierce and hopeful.

"It's very pretty, miss." She blinked, and I saw her face falling, but there was nothing I could do. I didn't think saying *sex* or *angry* to Miss Julia Hewitt was a good idea. She turned slowly away toward the window, frosted with its white ferns of ice.

Not long after that, I arrived at the Hewitts' on a day with no cars in the drive. I parked in the alley as usual, let myself in the back with my key, poured a cup of their leftover cooling coffee, and started my work, figuring myself to be alone. But an hour or so in, when I switched off the vacuum and knelt to turn it upside-down and pull strands of tinsel out of its rollers, I heard suddenly the sound of someone crying, high and bereft like a child cries. I followed the sound down the hall. When I knocked at Julia's door, the sobbing grew louder.

When I pushed the door open, she was sitting on the bed, her hands gripping her knees through her skirt. It was dark; the shades were still drawn. Her soft sweater was robin's-egg blue, and the usual pearls gleamed at her throat. Except for her face, which was wet and red and somehow distorted, she looked beautiful, just like the magazines: her blond hair back in a clasp, her smooth long hands with their pearly nails, her slender, unmuscled legs in pale stockings. She had no shoes on, though. Her loafers were kicked to the side, and her toes curled miserably into the carpet. She stared at me, her bud-mouth open.

"What is it, miss?" I whispered.

"What are you *doing* here?" she cried. She stared at me as if I were, in truth, a perfect stranger.

I began to feel nervous. I spoke carefully. Was she having one of the nervous breakdowns of which women sometimes spoke?

"I clean the house, miss. I'm Antoinette."

She shook her head.

"No, I know that. I mean *really*. What are you really doing here? Why am I sitting here, doing nothing?" It came out as a wail.

I thought of what telephone numbers I could call to get her mother home. The beauty parlor, maybe. I knew not to disturb Professor Hewitt at work. "You're home for the holidays, miss."

"She could do what you do. The house isn't even that dirty." She sobbed hard into her hands. "Why do we even need it cleaned up every week? Do you have children, a family of your own? Where do you even live?"

"Miss. Let me make you some tea." I put my hand on her arm, but carefully. I'd never touched a Hewitt.

"I don't *want* any tea," she shrieked. "Everyone's always making me tea, telling me to calm down. But how is tea going to help? There's no justice." Her body was heaving in time to her sobs. "There's no justice. How can everyone be so *calm*?"

It was 1965, and things had settled down some; people had stopped getting shot. News of the world outside North Dakota came to me only through the televisions and radios of people I worked for, and things sounded all right again. But *all right*, as every adult on the reservation knew, meant business as usual, which had never been good for us. Which I'd always thought rich white people liked.

Miss Julia and her qualms about justice: this was new. "Why are you here?" she cried at me. "The little things *do* matter," she said, as though continuing an argument that had started long before I'd entered. "Why does Mother make you park in the back?"

I sat down next to her on the bed. It was so soft. I took her hand and held it.

"I know, miss," I said. "I know." Our eyes met.

She reached over and clutched my hand in hers, and she leaned her head on my shoulder and kept sobbing until the sobs got smaller. We sat there, girls almost the same age, for a quarter of an hour. Her breathing slowed.

When I heard a car door slam, she didn't move. "Miss," I said, and shook her a little. She looked up, startled and sleepy. The crying had worn her out. "Why not take a little rest, miss? I'll tell your mother you're napping." She nodded, her face grateful and dazed, and I slipped out, shutting her door behind me.

I should not have been surprised. But I was.

A week later, Miss Julia's new diamond bracelet that she got for Christmas went missing. Her mother insisted that I'd always been trustworthy—that I and my mother before me were known never to steal—but Miss Julia said she'd seen me poking around in her things. Professor Hewitt stayed out of it, casting me sympathetic glances. Mrs. Hewitt said she would do me the kindness of not telling the other housewives if I would simply return the bracelet, which of course I could not do.

But then she didn't tell the other housewives anyway. I guess she had her own suspicions.

Over time, my money did it all. I have cleaned houses now for forty-three years, and I have seen the places in the photographs.

The world did not settle down, but I have stood on the observation deck of the Eiffel Tower and looked out over Paris with my own eyes. I learned to tango in Buenos Aires; I've crossed the Bridge of Sighs.

Miss Julia went back east to finish her schooling. She married, it was rumored, a black man and marched in protests. Later, they got divorced. She put all that behind her, as the ladies of Halford said to each other. She married a banker, had children, and lives in a big house in Connecticut to this very day.

I gave birth to twin sons in a house whose smoke my parents can see from their porch. The bedroom my boys shared has heat vents right in the floor. For college, they went out east, and people say they look like Gregory Peck. In warm weather, I stand on my porch and smell the breeze.

And always, I remember the frozen day I learned that rich people aren't happier—that the secret they struggle to keep is that they know the way things are is wrong. It rumbles unacknowledged under all their polished surfaces. Sometimes, it erupts.

I remember rich white Julia Hewitt and her beautifully groomed anguish in the darkened room where we touched. It was pain, and it was real.

But she was young. With age, they get used to it just fine.

The Small Heart

I met my third lover at an educational conference in San Francisco. He's from there and a Democrat, talkative, with short, messy brown curls and brown eyes, and we had sexual intercourse twenty-three times in four days the first time we met. I counted; it was a matter of pride. I'm forty-seven. I didn't know I had it in me.

Then he went home to his wife, and I flew back to Omaha and my husband, Bob, who keeps building decks off the back of our house. We have six decks, all at different levels, splayed out in various directions radiating from our back door. There's not much yard left. What he'll do when he gets to the fence, I don't know. He builds wooden planters at the edges of the decks to serve as protective barriers, for the grandkids or in case someone's not paying attention, so I fill them with flowers—annuals, which have to be replaced every spring. It keeps me busy. Sometimes while I'm out grocery shopping at the Hy-Vee, he jacks off into his used underwear. When I do the wash, I find them, glued in on themselves like shame.

The honesty of my third lover is what first struck me, the way he hid nothing about himself, nothing—and thus was, without trying, never predictable. What hit me next was the warmth, the soft heat of his candor, his utter ease with himself, his unwillingness to hide anything: his imperfections, bad habits, flashes of cruelty, smallness, selfishness, his odd fears or the moments of crazed expansiveness when he loved the world and everything in it, his ecstatic sufi-twirl of absorption in whatever it was—a street carnival, getting coffee, making marinara sauce—his rampant goofiness. With him, everything was visible, and in this, he was childlike: simple, direct. Lovable.

I'm made of plainer stuff. Neo-Puritan parents. My sister's a pro-life, full-time clinic-protesting, stay-at-home mom, and my brother's in prison for possession.

At the middle school where I teach, every other teacher on the faculty is (1) married, (2) Republican, (3) white, (4) Christian, and (5) overweight. Every female teacher I know is on an antidepressant of some kind. The men, who can say? The social studies teachers have military recruitment posters on the walls of their classrooms. This is Nebraska. No one, to my knowledge, is a pacifist or an anarchist, both of which I seem to find myself becoming in my quiet moments when I sip my green tea and watch the sun fall over the cornfields.

Bob and I have two grandchildren already, Angelique and Desiree, slutty sorts of names, it seems to me.

My third lover and I joked about baby names. I went to Sausalito and rented a houseboat for a week, and he told his wife he had to work late. We talked about politics mostly and how I'd voted for Nader and how none of the other teachers at my middle school even knew what the Green Party was until after the election was over. How when I was a kid my parents called me an idealist and a dreamer and beat me for it. How he'd met his wife in art school and she spent hours locked away making weird stuff with wire mesh and feathers and papier mâché about feminism and being a woman and then would cry in there but wouldn't open the door when he knocked.

"Bougainvillea," he said he'd like to name a daughter. Look at all the other names that come from flowers: Rose, Iris, Daisy. It was bougainvillea's turn. He'd call her Bo for short. For a while after September 11th he and his wife had been really close and he'd thought it was maybe finally time to start a family, but then she'd started closing herself away in her studio again, and he, who'd broken it off with the one before me, started wanting someone to talk to again and also fuck.

When I made love with him those twenty-three times in four days, I felt guilty but thought maybe it was just something you had to get out of your system if you'd been married a while. I had thought Bob Dole's speaking out would make a difference. Why I married a Republican I do not know. He can't admit to liking the porno hidden in his toolbox in the garage and turns away silent when I bring up Viagra. So I figured maybe I'd blown the carbon out of my engine with the conference in San Francisco. When I got back, I tried not to look at how Bob talked with his mouth full when we went out for steak on Thursdays. Sometimes then I couldn't even get interested in my appetizer, and I'd say to myself in my mind, "What kind of exotic blossom are you? Do you think this here's a hothouse?"

I'd use the vernacular like that, like it was my parents talking to me in my head, which happens anyway. I'd use their phrases. "What kind of princess do you think you are?" Like the princess and the pea story, which I loved as a child and my mother thought was stupid. But each fall when there's a clinic for flu shots at the school nurse's office, twelve dollars each, I'm the only one in my department who bruises up.

I'd look at that food moving in Bob's mouth and remember the times early on when we were making the kids and I'd be teaching the next morning and all of a sudden a final little worm of warm stuff would slip out into my underwear, which is very unnerving if you're talking to a room of seventh-graders. When the bell rang I'd hurry to the teachers' restroom and wipe, but when I'd pull my underpants up they'd be all icy and wet against me and I'd hate him.

And not know what to do. Because Bob's a good man, all the things they say: no vices, steady worker, everything a good woman wants. So I was the bad one for my boredom and I tried to think of a future in which I would really be fascinated by carpentry, which was after all the Lord's profession. No one sings at Sunday service as loud and heartfelt as Bob, and sometimes after I've cooked something he really likes for dinner, he cups my face with both hands and looks into my eyes and tells me I'm God's gift to him, and his eyes are so big and warm I have to change the subject.

I am a bad woman. My parents were right.

It was on the Internet I found the houseboat in Sausalito and it was on the Internet I sent an e-mail to my third lover with the dates of my arrival and departure, and so maybe what my sister says about computers and Satan is true. Each day my third lover would arrive at four o'clock, straight from the high school where he taught US history from a cultural studies perspective, and we'd stay in the houseboat until eight o'clock or so, when he'd shower and go home. By Wednesday I was getting restless with the same six positions, so during the day I found a Barnes & Noble and paid cash for the illustrated and updated *Kama Sutra*, and that carried us through Sunday, when I had to leave. I don't know what excuses he made up for his wife on the weekend, but he said she worked better anyway when he wasn't in the house at all, that she found his presence oppressive. We talked a lot between times. I liked it when I laid my head on his chest and he put his arm around me, because I didn't feel at all sheltered or protected. His arm was not massive, a manly arm to keep me safe from the big, bad world. It was just an arm, warm and alive.

The *Kama Sutra* I left on the houseboat nightstand.

Bob was hunting with buddies in Frontier County. It was Thanksgiving, and each of us had taken the whole week off. I'd made up an elaborate story about wanting to Christmas-shop in San Francisco just once in my life and see all the lights and the window displays in the fancy stores. Like, why not New York? Why not Chicago, which was closer? But Bob didn't think to ask that. I said how lonely I always got when he went hunting, so he'd feel guilty. Worked like a charm.

But I didn't see lights or window displays. In the mornings I walked along the rocky waterfront or took a taxi to the Muir Woods, where I learned it was redwoods I should have said I'd needed to see, not department stores. I felt small and alive in their shelter. Back in town, I'd sit outside with my hot tea at the open-air cafés and watch the people go by with their little dogs, and I'd fill my eyes with the colors and life: the blue of the bay, the mossy emerald green of the islands, the bright hues of all the flowers blooming. Palm trees. In November. Waves. Beautiful people smiling, jogging, walking with each other and chatting, pushing cute kids in strollers. Back at the houseboat, I'd take hot baths where I'd soak until I fell into a trance, my mouth open and half in the water, half out, sunk down into the wet warmth like a frog. With just a towel knotted around me, I'd stand on the balcony, my hands on the wrought iron rail, my knees clouded with hydrangeas. Little white boats would sail by. Waves would sparkle. The light would shift. And then my third lover's knuckles would knock on the door, and I'd stay in the bedroom with him until dark. After he left, I'd shower and walk to an Italian restaurant and eat alone, watching lights shimmer in the dark bay.

I had to buy some crap, I-heart-SF this and that, at the airport. I planned to tell Bob that the stuff in the fancy stores was just too expensive—to say that it was the experience of looking and shopping that I'd gone for, and I'd gotten that for free, and that I'd do my Christmas shopping at Target like every year—which I knew would come as a relief to him.

My mind debated. If it wasn't just sheer sex—if my third lover and I had talked, too, and had sex over and over with our whole bodies twined and pressed hard together and our eyes open—didn't that say something about whether or not I should stay married? Didn't that suggest at least a hint of love? I leaned my head against the airport window and watched the stars shift ever so slightly. By eight o'clock the next morning, I'd be teaching thirteen-year-olds, clad in my L. L. Bean no-iron skirt. Opaque hose from Target, suede slip-ons from Lands' End. Would it be poetry? Or sentence diagrams? I couldn't remember. Whatever the lesson plan said. Different from geometry, which Bob teaches to accelerated kids in eighth grade. "If you could just tell me *where*, and how hard, and how long," he said once, plaintive, sitting up, the lamplight shining on his paunch, slick with earnest sweat, his penis curled like an embarrassed comma on his thigh. His voice had a note like despair I tried not to hear.

I finally boarded the plane. While everyone was getting situated in their seats, I took out my cell phone and opened text messaging. I tilted it away from the woman in the next seat and typed a note with my thumbs to my third lover.

When I get home, I'm going to talk with my husband about moving out. If I can feel the way I feel with you, then there's no sense in going on with it all.

It has not seemed miserable to me all these years. But now I wonder if those other married people secretly had what you and I have had, and that's what gives them the courage to keep on with it all. I always felt our neighbors and the other teachers and the bright gerbil-eyed women at Bob's church like a pressure squeezing in on me from all sides, like a jello mold, shaping me into what there was space for.

But now I think maybe they're all having secret ecstasy. Without that or the promise of that, I don't think I can do it for much longer.

I was wondering how you felt about me, and seeing me again, and maybe seeing me for real. Just me. For the long term.

I didn't send it. I stared out the window. My thumbs were exhausted and sore. All that, and the stars had barely moved. I shut my phone down for takeoff.

When we lifted into the air, I felt real vertigo. I knew the power of words, how they could be irrevocable, how they could force me into being the unacknowledged legislator of my life. Within a month, I could be living in a green place, a place where flowers bloomed on their own, where a warm wind blew in from off the water, and the sun shone, and bookstores and coffeeshops and art galleries crowded together along winding streets. I could be making love with a man who knew how. It was a terrible temptation, a beautiful promise, and the fear of so much change and the confusion and pain I'd surely cause kept me from sending my note in haste.

But when the flight attendant handed me my ginger ale and little blue bag of pretzels, I knew suddenly that I couldn't stand to rip out the dried roots of impatiens one more year. I was tired of prettifying borders someone else had built.

When the plane landed, I stayed in my seat while everyone jostled and grabbed for the overhead bins and muttered while the door stayed shut and the plane grew warm. I opened my phone, found the text, and pushed send. While everyone else strapped on their paraphernalia, I sat with my hands over my cellphone in my lap. Probably someone would think I was trying to warm a bird to life.

In the town where I live with Bob, there hasn't been any racist violence since the seventies. Still, I don't know any black people or Jews, not personally—the occasional student, yes, but not adults, not as friends. We've got Hispanics moving in for factory and meatpacking jobs now, so sometimes I have students who don't know any English, but it's okay with me. Some of the other teachers just go nuts about it in the faculty lounge, but I think, *What if I moved to Mexico?* I wouldn't know any Spanish. I wouldn't want people to get all mad at me while I was learning.

I said that in a faculty meeting once and everyone looked at me like I was crazy, even Bob, and I shut up. A few nights later, he started asking tentatively if I'd been thinking of moving to Mexico when we retire. Because he'd heard you can live pretty cheap down there, with a maid and everything, the dollar's so much stronger.

No, I'm not thinking of moving to Mexico, I said.

But then I did start thinking of it. Someplace on water, away from everyone I know. The light. The bougainvillea tumbling over the patio walls. No maid, though. In fact, in my daydreams, there's no one but me and strangers.

There's a story I teach sometimes in my accelerated class about a high school boy, a debater, who gets dragged on the Million Man March by his dad, a drunk he's just bailed out of jail. It's a good story and class discussion goes well, but I pay to photocopy it myself because I'm not sure the school board would approve. I leave it off my lesson plan. The secret reason I teach it is because of these lines: "Outside, autumn is over, and yet it's not quite winter. Indiana farmlands speed past in black and white. Beautiful. Until you remember that the world is supposed to be in color." It's a key I slip secretly to the students; they can use it if they want, if they notice.

My third lover is an atheist. My first was Barry Hardesty, and we did it on a picnic table in the Sarpy County Pork Producers' Pavilion on the 4-H grounds. He kept talking about moonlight and my hair in an obligated kind of way. He was a Methodist. And then Bob I count as my second lover, just so my number isn't so low, and he's Church of God. I don't know what I am.

My breath went in and out of my nose in little shallow pats of excitement as I got my luggage. I stood in the heated shelter, waiting in the dark for the airport shuttle to come take me to the long-term parking lot, not checking my phone yet, wanting a solid seat under me when I did. I wondered if Bob had gotten home from Frontier County and if he'd gotten a buck and what we would say to each other when I got there.

The shuttle lurched up sighing, and I got on with three tired-looking businessmen and wondered if I looked too awake at this time of night in November, if my eyes weren't too shining or my cheeks more rosy than they should be after Thanksgiving.

We swayed sideways on our benches, and I pulled out my phone. No one was near me or interested so I held it on my knees as I opened everything up. It was like throwing turtle bones or sacrificial intestines or the I Ching. And there was his name in the inbox, waiting, and my breath caught in my mouth and hovered there. I thumbed his message open.

Suzy, baby. We've never been less than honest with each other, right?

I'm married. My wife & I, we have a life together. We want kids 1 day. She's a little depressed rite now while she figures things out, but I love her. I like my life.

U r a real sweetheart, Susie, u really r, but I'm 12 years younger than u, remember. I'm not looking for anything serious or permanent. If u r, then I'm not the 1.

Hope we can do it again sometime (if u r cool with that).

I clicked him away and dropped the little machine into my purse quickly, like a used wad of Kleenex. I clutched my hands together and then saw how tight they were and made them let go of each other.

I tried leaning my head back against the window, but it vibrated my skull. So I just sat straight up for a while and concentrated on keeping my brain very, very, very empty while the shuttle moved us through the darkness.

When its blinker clicked in the heated air with a metallic plink, I looked up, scanning for my station wagon, as we turned into the Park-and-Ride. Weirdly, the car was haloed by bobbing irregular shapes that glinted in the headlights. Purple, red, gold. Heart-shaped Mylar balloons. Like my old car was a float in some crazy parade.

And there was Bob, standing in his parka, beaming his hopeful smile. His pickup was parked next to the wagon.

The shuttle lurched and stopped, and all of us stood up hesitantly, holding onto the handrail, waiting to see if there'd be another lurch. But there wasn't. *I like my life*, my third lover had written.

I got my suitcase and put my folded dollars into the hand of the driver and said thank you, stepping carefully down to the asphalt. The balloons were a small bobbing splash of color in the lit square of the parking lot, which was only a small square washed with gray in the vast blackness of the Nebraska night. Heading for Bob, I tried to make my face look touched.

He had cut short his hunting trip for me. He had stood out in the icy wind to make this extravagant gesture in front of other people.

"Oh, Bob," I said as he took my bag.

"I did it," he whispered into my ear, his words rushed with excitement. "I saw Dr. Harring and got the prescription filled. Just like you wanted." He squeezed me hard, then pulled away to look at me and stroke my hair. "I love you, Susan Lorraine," he said, looking in my eyes, and he gathered me into his arms.

Bloody

My menses are upon me as I write, which is altogether fitting: this is a bloody story.

Write with your fingers dipped in woman's blood, smelling of iron, exhorted the wild French feminists of the sixties and seventies, those indecorous ladies. *Write with the milk of your breasts.*

But theirs were the days of fire and revolution, of students in the street and violence. Now we are tired. Now we have full-time jobs and full political participation and agendas chock-full of our full social lives. Now we are full unto vomiting; now we are busting a gut. Now we call ourselves *gals* and append the prefix *post* to our old commitments. Passionate calls for justice just exhaust us.

Now when I say my menses are upon me as I write and note that this is, in fact, a bloody story, I'm not metaphorically wiping divine, defiant, blah-blah woman-blood down the page in glorious crimson streaks of rebellion. I have cramps. I took a Nuprin to be able to sit here. The shared bloodiness of my crotch and my memories is mere, sheer coincidence, which I'm giddily, rampantly warping into the semblance of meaning by juxtaposition, arbitrarily jamming into some kind of metaphor, some kind of forceps-wrenched birth, because that's what artists get to do, and though I'm actually only a teacher at a woo-woo progressive private high school in San Antonio, I fancy myself an artist. Why not?

In 1991 I was twenty-five years old and living in Houston, that heat-oozing armpit of an urb. I was wondering what to do with my beamish and recently graduated self. With my bachelor's in sociology and a minor in women's studies with extra interdisciplinary coursework in postcolonialism and globalization, I had landed an excellent position in a coffeeshop.

It was very wonderful. There were so many magical kinds of coffee, so many myriads of idiosyncratic ways to prepare a single cup, that it sort of restored your faith in the world. Oh, the exotic names. Arabica. Oh, the tantalizing smells. Oh, the way foamed milk gums up your hair. Oh, the way total strangers call you by your printed name all day. Oh, the thousand ways a stranger's face can express impatience, even fury. Oh, how voluptuously do people sink into their rage. Sometimes I did incompetent stuff just to see them careen right up to the brink of socially acceptable behavior. And then I would just smile and slowly blink and talk very slowly but in a sweet way, like I was incapacitated but trying my best. I would watch them like my eyes were a camera and I was the documentary film director, capturing their inadvertently revealing moments for an audience of me.

Despite these diversions, my hours at the cozy little coffeeshop in a chicly landscaped shopping center near Rice, from which I'd graduated super-duper-cum-laude, did not form the center of my intellectual-emotional life. No. Rather, I read a lot. Had boyfriends. Went to museums, of which Houston has many. I loved museums even then and could spend all day by myself down on Bissonnet in the Museum of Fine Arts, moving incredibly slowly from one painting to another, sort of zoning out in front of them, waiting for them to open and chat me up a bit, each in its own particular way. Very Merleau-Ponty. Each piece would just sort of unfold, until all its hows became clear, lit, gelling into its why, and then its why would just suddenly vanish, just twinkle away, and it would just *be*. It would glow with its selfness, and I would revel in the faux-illuminated rot of people with a few hours of phenomenology and Asian religions under their belts. But whatever. That's what it was like.

And not just art. In the Museum of Natural Science, I would move slowly into the Cockrell butterfly room, the leaves and trees and sunlight all around me in the glassy air, and the rustle of a thousand wings, gold and orange and blue. My arms floated up of their own accord as all over me the papery creatures settled, the thin tickle of their black paws stippling my skin. I have stood there, humming softly, with my eyes closed, standing in the soft heated sunlight as in a state of grace, dazzled with the consciousness of their color all over me, suffusing me with the air's soft rush as they moved, until my arms grew tired. Their wings gemming my skin and clothes and hair.

And it's not only paintings and butterflies that do that, coincidentally, or so I would have sworn to you in 1991, feeling very holy and quite close to some important and ineffable breakthrough. No: anything could. A wooden bowl. A very ordinary tree. Anything to which I paid close enough attention.

But museums seemed like whole buildings designed to encourage the safe paying of attention, where it's okay, where it's not weird to slow up and look—whereas when I walked slowly sideways like that down a sidewalk, staring deeply at the hydrant, the fat urn planted with wilting petunias, the brass plaque of the law firm with its columns of names, the piss-drenched guy in the alcove of the closed-down department store—when I did that on the streets of Houston, that crabwalking laser-gaze, I got myself stared at and worse.

So museums were good.

I see that I've strayed from blood. Had you forgotten about

65

the blood? You had probably not forgotten but instead were growing impatient; my voice is probably not enough to carry you. *Is* it carrying you? Am I *likeable* as a narrator? Which is to say, am I a gratifyingly aspirational ego ideal with which you can nonetheless still readily identify, via my description of endearing flaws that resemble your own? Which is to say, do you want to be me? Because that, according to the focus group that's actually authoring this, would be really ideal. Moreover, does the whole idea of blood seem like too much of a downer for the viewing audience, or is it promisingly optimistic? I mean, give us blood, sure, but make it *optimistic*. *Redemptive* blood; we're all Jesus freaks under our jeans. Is this rupture of the vivid dream annoying? So very *done*, so very self-consciously pomo, and over, and we want something seamlessly retro now? Have I not noticed that American fiction has largely resisted the trend blah blah blah?

I'm just a schoolteacher. Cut me a break.

So, all right, fine, whatever, galloping onward toward the blood: in 1991 I stabbed my boyfriend *du jour* in the left shoulder and he lived, he was fine. They stitched him up at Houston General and he was fine. There was certainly blood, though, and plenty of it. I don't know what verb: *gushed*. It didn't spurt. The knife went in and out, and the blood was just suddenly *there*, soaking the shirt, flowing, red, real. Like the knife had opened the door to where a permanent flood was, to what was waiting all along: this red private flow, this shocking interior of my boyfriend, suddenly sacred and helpless, so different from the boyfriend I'd wanted to *kill*, the mean boyfriend, who'd done his usual condescending bullshit just one too many times, the boyfriend I had sincerely loved, and who'd eroded my happiness chip by chip, his casual chisel wedging into all my nervous weak points, and then the quick blows of his disdain.

The ambulance was very speedy, by the way. Perhaps because we sounded white. Perhaps because of our address. Perhaps because he yelled, "God damn it, Abby, give me the phone," in his gorgeous deep gravelly voice I had always loved, husky and ragged now with pain and desperation—actually, come to think of it now, all these years later, kind of sexy in its urgency—and I handed it over, and he said into the phone, "Jesus, get the hell over here, get over here now," and anyone, even a jaded dispatcher for the Houston PD, could hear the naked fear of a respectable, well-educated, middle-class, and outraged hip young white man, the sort I usually dated.

So that's how I went on trial and got psychiatrically evaluated and found out that maybe moving very slowly in a Zen-like trance from fire hydrant to wino was not a particularly deep artsy Rilkesque thing to be doing after all but actually, drum roll, the result of just a little ol' chemical imbalance! Easily remedied with medication! And a three-month stay in a psychiatric hospital! And I won't go there! Because it's been done! Fragile girls who drink too much or fuck too much or won't eat and end up on the ward have been done aplenty in both life and art, and Angelina Jolie won an Oscar for one of the movies and who can compete with her. Nobody. And I'm not the richest cutest woman with great comic timing who could swear to that. Oh, whoops! Generations to come will not know what I mean. Generations to come will need an earnest footnote researched and written by an earnest underpaid editorial assistant. To what extent may a high school teacher indulge in delusions of grandeur before she is actually, clinically delusional?

So here's what I learned: Right next to sanity, there is insanity, like a door you can open, if you push. Hell, I was walking back and forth through it all the time, like those swinging saloon doors in cowboy movies and my aunt Linda's kitchen, and I didn't even know it. Look at the faces of strangers, of parents, of the person you sleep with; you might see the crazies flickering. Who knew?

So now I am very, very careful. The tinkering has taken years. Now I am a delicate balance of expensively synthesized molecules. I am a miracle of calibration, a biochemical experiment that finally went right. Continuing caution required. Taking a Nuprin, for example, is not the blithe gesture it might be for another woman my age, staring childlessness in the face on the 22nd of yet another fucking month, and I do mean fucking, because we're nothing if not in earnest, my amazing, saintly husband and me.

I'm thirty-nine. And not ungrateful: a hundred years ago, I'd have been hanged for stabbing that boyfriend and totally missed my late twenties and thirties. Or I'd have been locked away somewhere with the other nutcases in a big unsanitary building, raped by wardens and drooling on myself.

This is much better: marriage to a good man, a sweet little house out in Bandera with a view of trees. I'm not complaining. But what with the infertility drugs and the previously existing chemical imbalance now remedied by a fat cocktail of interacting medications, taking a Nuprin is a *judgment*, a decision. Now I have to think about things, even popping a wee pill. And bigger things.

For example, I have to consider whether my eventual potential adorable bundle of joy might not turn out to be a genetic replica of my own psychiatric imbalance—though in The Future, I reassure myself, they'll know how to deal with that better; they'll have my dear little Sweet Pea safely drugged up by the age of three, if necessary. But I also have to consider how I'll cope in the meantime with what all those flooding pregnancy hormones may do, with what post-natality may do, and whether my doctors will be able to maintain my current level of functioning.

Besides which, there are days already when just watching the news—machete-severed stumps where children's limbs were, or Wolf Blitzer spewing his urgent bullshit—can make me utterly sure that the only rational thing to do is to stab everyone, or else stagger around muttering the names of herbs and wildflowers like the only names of peace, like Ophelia, wandering out and finding water willing to embrace me.

But the sweetly bloated corpse of a fragile-minded mama is not a legacy you want to leave a kid.

So I wonder how reasonable this ticking is.

Sometimes, when the house is quiet and I'm alone and I hear strange echoes of that old internal cackling, it occurs to me to wonder whether one day the dear little Butter Bean will drive Mommy right to the edge: whether one day I'll be making up some big nationally delectable lie about a black man and a carjacking while I cry extremely convincingly into the TV camera, and days go by while the police hunt, and interrogate me further, and my story starts to reveal inconsistencies, and my husband—my dear sweet trusting husband who knows all but keeps showing up anyway, my dearly beloved, my brave bad penny— while my husband, who has always believed me, suddenly finds himself walking very slowly sideways through the house, trembling, whispering *No, no,* staring deeply into household objects that could, he feels sure, reply: they could, they could reveal to him what's happening, reveal to him the truth, where his child is, where the good wife he knew and trusted has gone—

But the toaster, the counter, the espresso machine, they answer back nothing.

A Place I Shouldn't Go

I raise my hand and run spread fingers through my hair back from the temple napeward, laughing, and I know that I seem poised and assured because those are words people use about me, but inside I am trembling.

She laughs, too, and links her arm through her husband's on the other side of the kitchen counter. "It's such a lucky coincidence that your conference was here in Greenville," she says, and I agree with her. And I say it is so kind of them, especially at such short notice, et cetera, and she says, Oh no, it was no trouble at all, it was their pleasure—after all, the spare room just sits there—and so on while I look around, see the clutter of children's belongings strewn like signs of comfort. They love her, she is a good mother, you can tell.

She raises her wine glass to something he's said, and I look at her slender fingers in their rings and her slender throat in its necklace.

My room is pleasant, with a view of forest. The children are already asleep. I change into my swimsuit because she is eager for us to sit in the hot tub together. I don't know why she would want that, except perhaps to grind on my mind's eye the image of them sitting there together, the two of them, with their arms around each other and glasses of wine in their hands as the sun cries fire and sinks below the treeline. But really it isn't necessary. I've had it stamped on my heart from the moment I heard about their new whirlpool from a mutual friend: the permanent idyll, night after night, with the children all drowsy and tucked away safe and the bottle of good wine and then afterwards the good sex and a sound sleep.

But I go out anyway with a towel around me and I am proud of the way I look and move—strong, firm, with muscles and thews gleaming. Not like ten years ago, with the soft curves of youth and also youth's fragility. Now I am solid. But that's only my outside.

So we sit in the hot tub and my knees are careful not to drift and we chat about work mostly and a little about the children, and I am careful not to look at him too often, just once in a while, as one would look at a colleague in whose ideas one was not too terribly interested, not enough to cause comment later because I couldn't bear what he would say to reassure her. I couldn't bear her hissing quietly in the privacy of their room, *the way she looks at you*—and then his necessary responses, the reassurances, *it was a long time ago*, and the other banal exchanges they would have to make, but his words—*it meant nothing*—would break into shards and slide under the door to destroy me.

And I couldn't bear that and so I compliment them and point out squirrels and make inconsequential talk. And rather than waiting for the moment when we all get out and dry off and say things and perhaps look at one another wondering whether we should embrace or not and if so in what order and with what degree of enthusiasm and then decide not to after all and stand there knowing that we had decided, and knowing why—instead of waiting for that, I thank them and mention the early session and get out alone, my flanks dripping little silver beads. My strong legs lift and propel me out of there, leaving them in idyllic repose.

And I dry off in my room, proud of my body though I know

it is nothing to take credit for, if I'd had children certain things would be different about me too, but I cannot help it, a thin hot pride rises up in me because it's all I have, and I smear cream across my legs and belly in the darkness and lie on top of the sheets with the window open until I get cold and then I cover up and go to sleep. I dream in jolts and flashes.

And then I wake and cannot lie still. The bedclothes feel like straps binding me to the mattress. Water, I think. A drink of water. And I go to my door and push it open.

And I see him, across the broad room, past sofas and lamps, standing before the glass doors. His back is to me; he is looking out into the night, onto the deck, which is now swamped with silver, mysterious and gilded. He's gazing at the pool where we'd sat with water rushing and where now the water lies starless and still. The house breathes quietly with the safe hum of appliances.

He stands there looking out, his hands behind him.

I should not be here, I should not be in this place. I have come, against my better judgment—just one night, I thought. One night. I should not have come. The way he used to kiss me, softly, terribly, until I learned that kissing could be more than lips rubbing together for pleasure, more than tongues' arousing slide: how you could be possessed by the craving to know someone, to breathe him. But you know his hunger for security and that you yourself are no better, for all your bravery how tired you are, and you understand how he could never have chosen you, you who had nothing at all.

Twelve years ago I was young and my heart rushed out dumbly, but now my heart is layered and smart, and yet still, still I would rush to meet him. I'm held in the doorway only by the thinnest rein of decency, thin already and thinning further each time his hand clasps and unclasps around his wrist.

The pool he sees I cannot see, silent and still where it had whirled. I cannot see the picture he will keep: the water placid, me gone. He will keep it, superimposed over the image of my arm, my hand lounged across the sprawl of redwood planks, fingering the wine-stem. Still water will be layered over my smile, my polite glances, my hair dampening to ringlets, my breasts lifting from the thick warm water opaque with foam. This imprint, this smooth unbroken surface in the dark, will push down my red-strapped shoulders, shove my brown throat under, drown them in the depths.

And the image left for me? His hand, clutching and unclutching in the empty room.

The next morning I rise early. I write my distant note of thanks and am gone before the household wakes.

The Noren

Jim brought a noren back with him from his trip in Japan. He hung it in the doorway between the kitchen and the living room, claiming I had to do like the Japanese and pretend not to notice him working in there while I was in the kitchen, that I wasn't to interrupt or ask him about whatever project he was working on.

I like it. It's a nice bright print on rough blue cotton: Hokusai's famous wave, the eighteenth view of Mount Fuji.

I would stand in the doorway sometimes when the house was empty, reaching up to finger its hem where it hung just above my head. Sometimes, if I was a little tired or something, I would lean my forearm on the doorframe and my forehead against my arm. It's a position I've learned to recognize. I think I know what it means.

It's the principle of the noren that operates in Gothic, Colorado. We went out this year like we do every year, from the middle of May to the middle of August. I didn't do as many drawings this year. I'm not sure why. My prints and cards sell like crazy down in the little general store. Jim says I don't ask enough. As if I were in it for that . . . But really I couldn't find anything to draw. How many five-by-seven glacier lilies can you do, really? Columbine, monkshood, bottle gentians, scarlet gilia—

I'm no good at distance. I tried to draw Mount Gothic, looming up over us like an overdone backdrop, too intense for believability, really—you can't quite stand to look at it, to let that enormity be part of your everyday days. Anyway, that effort was a waste of good rag paper. Then I thought maybe a different perspective would do me good, so I hiked up it one day, toward the patches of snow near where the old woman is buried. Jim and I used to hike it together all the time, years ago. But anyhow I took my pad and pens and a water bottle and spent half the day getting up there. It's a good view of the lab. I thought I could maybe sketch the whole thing: the cabins, the laboratories, the general store and the library, the little outhouses like wooden commas tucked into the green. Our cabin. Twenty-three years it's been, every summer faithful like a clock, except the year we had to leave early to have Davey. The pines cradling it, the shed beside with Jim's equipment . . . But I flubbed it something awful. My hand just has no feel for faraway things.

Oh, it came out all right. Jim thought it was just fine.

But like a draughtsman's rendering.

There used to be so many flowers that I didn't know. Seeing one enough to draw it right just left me eager for the next. But now it's not that way. Jim says, so draw the marmots, draw the chipmunks. Draw the hummingbirds, he says. But I'm no animal charmer. They won't hold still long enough for me to see them. And hummingbirds? I'm a slow study. A flower waits for you, opens to you. You can touch it lightly when your eyes don't understand. But magical things that buzz and whir at you when you wear red? Wings you can't even see?

We don't have literal norens here, of course. But so many of the people come just for a summer, and the cabins are hardly equipped with the comforts of home. So in place of curtains we hang respect at the windows: no watching, please. Pretend not to notice. Of course, I sewed curtains for our own cabin years ago, and every spring we unpack them from the locked plastic crates with the pillows and bedding and rugs. But most of the cabins don't have them, and averted eyes are the unspoken rule. I've never looked before.

This year one of the graduate students had a friend up to visit. Jim likes the boy—Evan Summerlin, population biology, from UC somewhere, I forget. Jim's asked him before to help on the hummingbirds. But Evan's all for ants. Ant farms in his bedroom. Anyhow, he's a good-looking boy and bright and we've always had a good time trying to guess which of the girls will end up with him each summer. This year it was Andi, a sweet thing, pretty and strong the way a lot of the girls are now, and willing to talk him into a corner in the dining hall in front of everyone if she felt the urge. I liked watching that. She could talk a strict logic.

Anyway this other friend of his came up, a young woman from Texas, also pretty, and towing a little kid with her, a girl of maybe five. We had to pass her cabin on our way down the hill, and she and the daughter would be sitting out on the porch coloring together or playing clapping games and singing. She never came down to the dining hall, but Jim asked Evan about her. She was around Evan's age, I guess, but she had her degree already and was teaching history at Austin. Just a lecturer for now, but after all that's how Jim started. One of those women nowadays that does everything and does it well and still manages to look good doing it. Lithe and sweet like one of the aspens, with a thick gold braid like a rope down her back.

To tell the truth, I was a little intrigued, wondering to Jim over coffee if maybe there wasn't something romantic going on— if maybe she hadn't come out for more than the scenery and been disappointed to find Evan already attached. Or if maybe that little girl . . . I watched, but there didn't seem to be anything like that. Mornings, she'd be striding down the hill with a pack on her back and the baby in her arms, off for a day's hike. I never did see a woman more reluctant to put her child down, I'll say that. They held each other all the time, always stroking each other's faces and whatnot. Always laughing—the woman would dash around like a kid herself, playing tag games and hide-and-go-seek down in the valley by the road.

That little girl charmed everyone. Hannah, her name was. A sweet-cheeked little thing that promised to be pretty like her mother. She'd hop around the general store chirping questions and petting the stacked t-shirts while her mother paid for orange juice. Sometimes Evan would be done out at his site and come back early. He'd carry the little girl on his shoulders and call himself a bear, growling and staggering until she squealed. Sometimes the pretty girlfriend Andi would join the three of them, and that's when I really took note, but watching for tension was like watching for rainclouds early in the morning: pointless. Out here, if it's going to rain, it's just going to rain, and it's certainly not going to tell you about it ahead of time.

That's about as far as my watching went. I'm generally not one to pry. When I bought Jim a diary for Christmas, though, I bought him one with a lock: no sense setting up temptation where none needs to be.

One night, Jim had gone upstairs to bed and I was sitting up reading like I usually do. I've got one of the diaries of Anne Morrow Lindbergh, and I've been reading that. How about it? She has a wonderful education, loving parents, she marries a famous hero that she loves. She does everything just right—and has her first baby son stolen and murdered. How do you pick up a life after that? The one I'm reading is about their second little boy and how they moved to England to find a safe house, anonymity. Some of the passages just stun me in the heart and I have to look up and hold the teacup hot in my hand and struggle the wet burning feeling away.

I was looking up like that, stunned and unseeing, right at the woman's cabin, when I saw movement. My eyes refocused. Through the upstairs window, I could see Evan and the little girl wrestling. I couldn't hear anything, of course, but they were plainly laughing and giggling and yelling up a steady stream of silliness. Real cute. The woman was dark in the yellow light of the downstairs window, washing dishes. Smoke wisped from the chimney. The night was blue and cold.

Suddenly, as I watched, the woman let go of the tin cup she was washing. I watched it drop. I thought of its slow fall through the soapy water and the clink it would make as it settled against the porcelain. Her arm went up and leaned from elbow to wrist against the metal cabinet just above, and she let her head drop forward until her forehead rested on her arm. Her hand glistened, and suds dripped down to the sink. She paused, as if waiting for a signal, and then her face twisted up, her skin screwed into roads of hurt, and she began to wail. Her shoulders convulsed as she leaned there wailing and sobbing. I glanced upward, but Evan and the child continued to wrestle and play, and I realized then that she was doing her crying in private, silently.

I felt an urge like panic. Should I get Jim? Should I go down there? I could. I could rap quietly at the door and take her by the arm when she opened it, lead her quickly out under the moon and away from the laughter. I could talk to her in the voice women use with each other when we're alone at night and out of doors, and she could cry out loud and I could comfort her. The pine grove—I could show her that. It's a good place for sorrow.

But even while I was choking to my feet in a blur of pain and recognition, I saw her straighten abruptly and wipe her eyes with a dishtowel. Her lips forced a curve, and I glanced higher to see what she had heard. Evan had swung the child onto his shoulders and was beginning to thump down the wooden stairs. He disappeared with the girl. Another attempted smile on the woman's face, and by the time they entered the room she had gotten it right and had turned. She was smiling, I could see by her profile. I watched for another minute. They all kept saying things and smiling, and then I got up and drew the curtain.

The Tasting

This one time the bartender where I worked took me to a wine-tasting, the sort where you do swallow the wine and eat hors d'oeuvres from trays. Tickets were fifteen dollars each, which seemed like a fortune, when the boys I liked just sat around dormitories getting stoned or drove out to state parks in their old Toyotas and camped on bare rock. So I was flattered. The bartender was nice with blond hair, and his car had everything automatic. At the tasting, we walked around in fancy clothes among other dressed-up people, and he kept saying, "Oh, have another one. I'm driving."

I didn't hold liquor too well, and when he said I seemed a little woozy and he'd take me back to his apartment until I felt better, I thought, *Well, that's very considerate.*

"You can lay down in the bedroom," he said, and so I lay down on top of his bedspread in my dress and shoes, and the strange dark ceiling rocked slowly above me, leaning and listing like a boat on chop.

And then there he was on the bed as well, lying beside me in only a pair of red running shorts and rubbing his hand slowly over the front of them. I could hear the crisp sliding sound of his hand on the nylon, and it pushed me into nausea. I made it to the bathroom before I threw up, and then I hung there for a while on the edge of his toilet, which I was grateful to see was pretty clean for the toilet of a guy who lived alone. No rusty band of yellow wavering below the rim.

He came in after a while and helped me up and chatted amiably while I cleaned my mouth with toothpaste on my finger. His chest was broad with blond hair on it, and he kept looking at it in the mirror while he talked.

He helped me back to the bed, where the sheets were now turned down, and I eased backward until I was prone again. The ceiling seemed more familiar now, friendlier, more of a traveled territory, and I felt my breath go in and out with a kind of comfort.

"Look," he said after a minute, "how about just a blow job, then?"

I groped to sit up. My feet found my shoes. Then I wove on my stupid heels into the living room. It was the days when phones were large stationary objects that sat sensibly on furnishings—endtables, kitchen counters—so I navigated my way to one and dialed for a cab company.

He said pissed-off things at my back while I watched out the window for the taxi. It wasn't a good part of town.

Then I left.

At work, he didn't look at me anymore or say hello.

A Favor I Did

So one night after a bad shift, all four of us went to The Blue Moon, a gay bar, so we wouldn't get messed with: me, Dolores, Rosie, and the new white girl, Alison, who was just at the restaurant for the summer. Alison came from Alamo Heights; she was home for the summer from a school called Vanderbilt—even its name sounds rich—and she was just waiting tables for spending money because her New Zealand trip didn't work out. The rest of us were there for life.

The rounds started coming, and Alison sat next to me. She was a nice girl. She had light brown hair and large dark eyes, and her skin was pale and smooth. Even without makeup, her cheeks were pink. She looked like Heidi in a kid's book.

As a waitress, she was not so good. She got confused and forgot things, and we all thought, *This goes to college?* but she was sweet to people.

Once I went to the walk-in for some lime juice and she was crying in there. She looked at me and wiped her fingers down her cheeks.

"It's nothing," she said.

"Okay," I said.

Hours later, after the restaurant had shut down for the night, we were stocking sugars together and she said meekly, "Iréne? I just wanted to tell you. When I was crying in there? It was just that table four had been very mean." Like I had been wondering about it all that time. Like I had been concerned. That was Alison: she thought people cared.

So it got late at the Blue Moon, and our hair got full of smoke. We drank and talked loud over the music and got rid of the feeling of waiting on people. We got up to dance and sat down to sweat, and I was starting to feel the exhaustion and starting to think about my mom asleep on the couch in my apartment while the girls slept, and what she'd say to me in the morning. Guilt was starting to put me in gear, and I reached for my bag.

But then Alison slid into the booth and sat next to me again. She sat there for a while, sipping her frozen margarita and telling me things about herself. Her boyfriend at school, his family, how they were doctors. Riding horses and oh do I know how marvelous it feels, sailing over a jump on a really fine animal? Oh there's nothing like it, you feel so free. I drank my Dos Equis.

She was a nice girl. It's not that I didn't like her: I liked her. I wanted my girls to have the things she had. It was what I worked for. So they could have smooth skin, a forehead with no worry in it, college. Boyfriends you haven't slept with yet. They were going to have all that, I would make sure. None of this being a stripper and dropping out of SAC because you're pregnant and waiting tables for the rest of your life.

Another round came, and Alison laughed and gave the guy a credit card that was her father's, and when he brought it back, she signed without looking. I watched her and drank my beer and waited till her soft voice stopped confiding. I put my hand on her shoulder.

"Do you want to know how I got my Mercedes?" I said. It's a '72 and needed body work and a paint job, and then a new engine. What's inside now isn't even Mercedes. But when I idle in front of the big front doors at the Catholic school to pick up my girls, with a dark bun and sunglasses and my manicured hands on the wheel, the other parents and the teachers look twice. Framed in the window of a dark green Mercedes, I look like a Bond girl grown up, a rich man's wife. My girls get in like the daughters of rich men. No one can touch them.

Did she know how I'd got that car?

"No," she smiled. Suddenly a mild alarm dawned on her face, like she was just realizing how much she'd talked about herself and was wondering if she'd been rude. I let her wonder. "How?" she asked, anxious to be polite.

I asked her if she knew a certain city councilman, an old guy with an apartment on the Riverwalk—to be close to the people, as he said. A white guy, in a wheelchair? She said she didn't know him but maybe her father did.

"I did him a favor," I said. My hand was still on her shoulder, and her hair fell against it. It was soft and slippery.

"What?" Her eyes were alert now. She looked excited, worried, like a scandal was about to be revealed, like maybe I'd sold him drugs or bought the votes of my illiterate neighbors. I leaned close. I could smell her. She smelled like flowers and clean sweat.

"I went to his apartment," I said. "I took my clothes off, and I got down on my hands and knees." Her eyes widened—I could see the pupils expand like ink dropped in water—and then a little click happened in them, like the worst had been confirmed, like I was on the other side of a great divide, and she would always be safe from my sort. But I kept telling it. "I crawled across the floor to him." My bent knuckles dragged up the back of her neck. "I knelt by his wheelchair," I said, threading my fingers through her hair, "and I blew him." She winced suddenly, and I softened my hand against her. "Sorry," I said. Her skull fit in my palm like a cup. "He called me Maria."

"That's not your name," she whispered.

"Hey," I said. "No shit." Her face was close to mine; there was the smell of lime and liquor. "He called me Maria and slapped me. Then he gave me the cash," I said. I took a drink. I was shaking from the alcohol and from being so tired. "Three times I went there and did it," I said.

Her eyes were frightened and I could see her lip trembling. Her pupils were huge and I could see her in them and I could see myself reflected. Then I hated her.

"You don't know anything," I said in a voice low and tight. My throat ached, I thought I would cry. I leaned closer, gripping her head the way a man grips a woman's. Her lashes flickered and her lips opened like in a movie when you know they're going to kiss. "You really don't know anything," I breathed hot onto her mouth.

How Winter Began

Dressed, I don't know how I stumbled home. My hands shook in the bitter dark as I tried to force the key. When it slid in, I opened the door to a house of silence.

I woke on the bed, blouse open, the little cups of my bra pushed aside. My skirt was bunched under me. When I pressed myself where it hurt, blood came away on my hand. My legs trembled. When I turned my head, my lips brushed piled coats.

"It's so loud," he said. Around us, people were dancing or yelling in knots of three or four.

"Yeah," said the one with green eyes. "Let's go someplace we can talk." He waved toward the stairway. Its carved wooden balustrade coiled at the top and unfurled downward, silky under my hand.

"You're gorgeous," they kept saying. There were three. When I tried to be funny, they laughed. They laughed at the things I said.

"You want another shot?" said the one with tan hair. "I'm getting you another shot."

In the marble-tiled foyer, I hesitated, nervous, happy. Everyone was talking loudly over loud music. Susi, who's always braver and already a senior, laughed her way into the kitchen, where the keg was.

In her bathroom, we glued lashes on with tweezers, brushed glitter on our shoulders. Susi tugged the rubber bands off my braids and raked her fingers through my hair.
"These gotta go," she said. "Way too high school."

"It's just Susi's, Mom," I said for the third time, throwing my stuff in my bag. "And her parents will be there all night." I had promised to call home in the morning, but she made me promise again. "Jesus, Mom. You're so paranoid."
Bundle up, bundle up, she kept saying, but it wasn't even cold.

Under Things

When I was putting myself through college and then medical school, my parents were estranged from me. They did not approve. It was the nineties, but still they wanted me to settle down with some nice local boy and raise a passel of grandkids and bring potatoes au gratin in a casserole dish to church dinners. Instead I left Kansas for good.

Despite our estrangement, they still saw their way clear to call once in a while when they needed money. Titus fell down the stairs to the cellar and broke his foot: Could I help out with the ER bill? Or it was Christmas and they needed to keep the heat on.

I tried to explain that going to school didn't mean I had money. Often the fridge in my studio apartment in Cambridge held nothing but boxes of pancake mix and a couple of spongy potatoes. The cupboard held stacks of black-and-white packs of generic ramen. I would ration it all out, like I rationed out sleep and long-distance minutes. When I called home once a week, the dutiful eldest daughter, I tried to explain all that.

But my family was unconvinced. To them—to their neighbors and friends and churchfolk and everyone they knew—college was still something for rich kids on TV. Med school, in and of itself, conferred wealth upon a person. By choosing education, I'd catapulted myself into that strange world beyond them. I must therefore be living, however inexplicably, beyond their means. About this, they were devout.

My college friends sold their books and CDs when things got dire, but I didn't have even those, so I sold plasma and sent that money home. I envied my guy friends, who had sperm to sell. My furtive rubbings' little dampnesses had no fiscal worth. I was the only one who cared whether they happened or not, and there were times, during med school and then residency, when I was far too tired to bother.

When I got my ob-gyn license, I took a position as the junior practitioner in a small clinic in Lowell, where I attended mostly working-class women.

I was gentle. I had too good a memory of the time my mother took me to a man she'd said was the dentist, after I'd gone to her, scared about the blood in my underwear. This was the eighties, but our school didn't have sex ed, and I started before my friends did, so no one in my circle was talking about periods yet. Though eleven, I'd never been to a dentist, so I didn't know what to expect, but stripping down, tying on the paper dress, and locking my heels into the metal rests seemed like a weird way to prepare to have my teeth examined. I lay there alone, waiting, my privates tilted into the air, feeling my teeth with my tongue and wondering. When the man came in with his lubed, gloved fingers and a metal contraption and put them up me, I screamed and could not stop screaming. I had to be tranquilized.

When my women's studies professor informed us (at the illustrious institution that scholarshipped me into education, like shoehorning me into too-tight shoes) that we were the children of privilege and that it was our obligation to make a difference and asked us to write down on index cards the difference we were going to make, based on the things in our own lives we wanted to change, I made my decision.

So in our little examining rooms in Lowell, I explain everything before I do it. I warm the speculum. I move slowly and say, "Are you okay?" a lot. Often the women cry before and after when we sit in the chairs to discuss things. Some cry during the exam, silently, their hands clenched around the blue vinyl sides of the table padding, their open eyes locked on the poster of flowers I taped to the ceiling. "Yeah," they say through their teeth when I ask if they're okay. I keep books in my office about sexual abuse and rape and post-abortion and post-natal depression for the patients who need to borrow them. In Lowell, there's plenty of sexual grief to go around, and sometimes I wonder if ob-gyns everywhere keep boxes of tissues at the ready in each room. Infertility treatments are where the money is, and my few Lowell patients who can afford those cry about that, too.

The only really good part is monitoring and delivering wanted pregnancies. I love that. The joy. I wonder if my mother had ever been like the women I treat, hopeful and soft before I was born. In my earliest memories of her, she'd already had four children, and her face stayed tired and sour.

When the expectant mothers come to the clinic, they sometimes bring their husbands, so I wonder, too—given my schedule—if I'll ever find time to meet someone who'll hold my hand during a sonogram, who'll gasp and look into my eyes the first time we hear the fast pulsing swish of our baby's heart.

After my dad passed, my mom softened up some. She was lonely, I think. Once I'd gotten settled in Lowell, she wanted to come up and visit. I demurred at first, thinking of her constant criticism and suspicion when I was a teenager, and then her skeptical long-distance questions about my faraway life. Finally, I relented. Maybe this could be okay. She planned at first to take the 'Hound, but Riley County to Lowell is a twenty-six-hour haul, even without stops, so I sent her a plane ticket and picked her up at Logan.

My old Jetta is hardly a doctor's car, and my little house was still spartan. Thinking to front-load my financial pain, I'd signed a fifteen-year note; if all went according to plan, I'd pay off my student loans, seventeen hundred dollars a month, in ten years, and then the house. Then my whole salary would be mine. I could give my mom whatever she'd need as she got older, and help out my brothers and sisters. I would have, at last, some of the things in the women's magazines in the waiting room: travel, beautiful clothes, interesting shoes. Spa trips. Fifteen years: not so long in the scheme of things, considering how many generations it usually takes to get out of poverty. As a high school senior, I hadn't grasped the magnitude of what I'd set out to do, which was probably a good thing: I'd been undaunted. And now I was halfway there.

I loved my tiny house. Everything about it was neat, compact. Everything worked. It wasn't the kind of grandiose money pit I'd seen my med-school friends buy, with soaring ceilings, and bay windows with window seats, and ruined parquet floors, which they repaired and refinished and refurbished, stocking the rooms with chandeliers from Anthropologie and dining room suites from Williams-Sonoma Home as they banked on their surgical futures.

In my house, everything was small, reachable, and my practical furnishings came from Ikea and Target and looked just fine, thank you very much. If the roof ever did leak, I could climb up myself and patch it. There was no crumbling mortar. In my tiny half-basement, no swags of old wiring sagged from the ceiling; its walls were coated with waterproof sealant and painted white, and the washer and dryer sat on a yellow braided rug.

Everything was within reach, under control. Everything smelled of Pine-Sol and Comet. Safe, tidy, clean.

"Hmph," my mother said, a noncommittal and nerve-wracking sound, as she considered each component of my fragile new life. I wasn't sure if she doubted my success or my frugality. I took her to our clinic. "Kinda small," she said. In my office, she spent a long time in front of my diplomas, inspecting. "Hmm," was the sound she finally made.

We had a week together, and I'd been setting aside some of my pay for the last couple of months so we could have a nice time. I'd cleared my schedule: we went out to dinner, to a movie. We went for walks.

Over meals, we talked about our relatives, about friends I hadn't seen in ten years. We talked about the war, and that was strange. She repeated what she'd heard on Fox News or read in the Letters section of her local paper, and I regurgitated what I'd gleaned from skimming the *Times*, the *Globe*, and BBC.com, trying to make it sound as if the analysis were my own and not from some op-ed column I'd read. Red state, blue state—like a Dr. Seuss title, our disconnect nearly that absurd. Our views glanced off each other, meeting for an instant of shared fact and then sliding quickly away into separate orbits of opinion.

But she actually knew people whose sons and daughters had died, while I'd long ago lost touch with my high school friends who'd joined the military. In a way, that was one of this war's larger truths.

"If you'd asked me a year ago did I support it," she said, "I'd have said yes. No question. Get rid of all of 'em over there. But now, I don't know." She paused, pushing her food around. Her eyes were sad and wistful. "I used to like that George."

We went to a coffeeshop, and she drank her first latte. At thirty-two, I'd never had a professional manicure, but I took my mother for one, and I watched as she closed her eyes and sighed, smiling, while the manicurist smoothed cream up her knotted forearms. Feeling pathetic and voyeuristic but unable to help myself, I gazed at her prolonged smile. Her white hair hung around her shoulders unstyled and yellowing at the ends, but she refused a cut and color. She admired my own hair, though, sliced in its practical bob. Once, in my kitchen, she reached out and stroked it, and I stood still like an animal, holding my breath, until she dropped her hand and turned away.

The week went by faster than I'd expected, and before I knew it, it was her final night with me. Her flight left the next morning at seven, which meant getting her to Logan by five: an early, groggy drive and goodbye. We were both, I think, perversely prolonging the evening, staying up later than was good for either of us. Warmed and emboldened by our good week together, I puttered around with little chores I could have left undone, and she tailed me through the house, chatting. I did dishes, and she dried and put away. When I told her it was more sanitary to let them air-dry, she just sighed and kept toweling them off, stacking them on the counter.

Then I had clean laundry to fold, so she followed me down to the tidy half-basement where the washer and dryer stood gleaming neatly side-by-side. Lifting the sweet-smelling clothes into the basket, I thought of her frigid cellar back home, where the battered, begrimed old appliances stood propped on cement blocks in case of rain. I remembered the mildewed stink of it. When I closed my eyes, I could see the bare bulb swinging in the dark room, like in a horror movie, the place where the serial killer keeps his victims alive.

My own little basement was well lit. I carried the rumpled warm clothes up the stairs, Ma still shadowing me, and flicked the light off.

In my bedroom, I put the basket on the bed, and we stood in the lamp's glow, me folding and smoothing. She stood near me, watching each move. My gold tiger cat Buster—a new indulgence, and what my mother would once have called a ridiculous waste of money on cat food and vet bills—lay stretched on the bed, doling out his contented, blinking, amoral stare. He was the first pet I'd ever had.

Sometimes, sitting alertly upright, staring at me, Buster reminds me of little blue-suited Tom Kitten from the Beatrix Potter book, which I'd recently read in the Lowell Public Library. I went every Saturday morning and asked the children's librarian to recommend children's classics, which I read in order by age, as though I could somehow, retroactively, remedy the lacks of my childhood. I'd started with *Good Night, Moon* and *The Runaway Bunny* and had worked my way through as far as the five- and six-year-olds' books; the elaborately illustrated covers of *Black Beauty* and *Anne of Green Gables* lured me onward. Sometimes my greed astonished me. It had no limits. I would have what others had had; I would give it to myself. I would restore to my psyche the things I'd missed. A childhood of safety and charm. Tired from work, I'd more than once drifted off at night staring at the little pictures of animals who talked and wore pinafores. I'd wake up groggy, my mouth thick with sleep and the book fallen open on my throat, and grope to switch off the lamp. I dreamed of animals waltzing in forests.

Sometimes Buster's sociopathically blank expression looks like Tom Kitten's, and other times, when he sits up and stares at me, it looks like Hannibal Lecter's, staring at Clarice, head tilted slightly to one side, body utterly still in his dark cement cell. Cats can be weird, unnerving, in an empty house at night. I'd have to pick Buster up then, and flip him over and bend my face to nuzzle him, to make him just a fuzzy cat again, purring.

"So tell me why you got this," my mother said, fingering a pale pink bra still curled in the basket. I looked away.

"There's nothing to tell." But there was; there was a story about it, a small but sweet triumph. How did she know? I felt shy. My mother, noticing me.

"Tell me," she said.

I hesitated, opened my mouth, began. When I'd passed my written specialty boards right after the completion of my residency, I took it as a sign of security, permanence, arrival. I took myself to Victoria's Secret.

It's true that women friends of mine found Victoria's Secret cheap, loud. I knew that. But they'd grown up comfortable.

For me, clad my whole life in cheap white cotton underwear, three to a pack from the drugstore—to me, who wore my period-stained pairs until they shredded, until the elastic gave up and just sagged along for the ride—to me, Victoria's Secret was a luxury emporium, a feathery flight into a kind of dreamy heaven of soft colors and satin. It was more than I had ever let myself afford.

A clerk measured me for the right-sized bra, of which I bought four, and then I chose seven pairs of matching underwear, so I had enough for a whole week without doing laundry. They weren't red or black, like underwear gifts from boyfriends—not the lacy or mesh or peekaboo things they were always so excited to give you. These were all smooth pale pink and cream, all matched sets, which I'd never had before, all discreet and comfortable, satiny, beautiful, like ice cream scoops, like the private garments of a well-cared-for daughter, a girl clean and well-kept all the way down to the skin, a person with nothing to anxiously hide. Not ragged, faded, torn. Not thin and rough. Not cheap to begin with, then falling apart.

Clean. Pale blossoms. Smooth. Shining.

I told my mother this as I continued folding, my eyes and hands busy. When I finished talking, I glanced at her. Without realizing it, I had lifted a pair of the cream panties into the lamplight, like some kind of Exhibit A. I dropped them back into the basket, embarrassed. It all seemed so personal. So little and stupid. I had paused to enjoy one definite moment of success, of security I'd earned myself, and I'd gotten soft things on the promise of my own hard work.

And just as the women's magazines swore they would, they'd quietly changed me. Though buying all that loveliness had made me sick with nerves at first—at the counter, handing my credit card over, I'd swayed, suddenly hot and dizzy, and thought I would faint—now when I put them on each morning, I feel good, cared for. A kind of soft pride had grown in me like a small watered plant.

I had shared this with no one, up until now. Perhaps my mother, a woman who'd lived poor all her life, would understand.

I looked shyly, hopefully, at my mother's face. More than anything, I wanted her to witness my act of largesse toward myself and approve, to say *Yes, sweet girl, you deserve that.* To bestow some kind of maternal benediction.

In that moment by the bed, I wasn't a doctor, or a proud single female homeowner with her own box of wrenches, or a durable young woman who'd made it on her own. In that moment, telling the story had made me just a daughter in lamplight, eager for my mother's love. I looked at her lined face and felt a hope that softened me.

"Well, one thing for sure," she said. "Don't you ever let me hear you bitch about money again."

Whore for a Day

For years, the bowl with its brimming crystal lip rested in the dark shelter of my aunt Ofelia's highboy. When Aunt Ofelia grasped the brown electrical cord and thumbed the cabinet's recessed bulbs to light, her rose-edged porcelain cups and plates and figurines leaped into gleaming life against the mahogany. They were pretty. But nothing whispered to me the way the bowl did. Its cut and frosted crystal sang of Iceland, Norway, of crisp, bitter winds, the smells of green moss and water, and glimmers in the dark, of (and here my imagination took further flight) a true and brilliant love, a wintry test of will that my pure heart would surely pass, my face framed in silver fur and rosily aglow.

Nine years old, I'd press my face to the highboy's panes and lose myself in the bowl's cold promise of beauty. My nose and breath and fingers would print the glass. Later, I'd hear my aunt muttering as she wiped the mess I'd left, her ropy arm muscling the rag in quick circles. Because the highboy held her treasures— the pretty dishes we never used, the little china people she could arrange at will—it was sacrosanct.

Like me, my aunt believed in talismans, the power of the forbidden, and being magically swept away.

But she was not a sharing woman. She never let me touch anything inside the highboy, never opened it in my presence. To this day, I don't know where she hid its key. Believing herself trapped, she couldn't see the jailor she'd become.

In our actual and daily life, we sweated in the bright heat of Miami. After her shift at Walgreen's, Aunt Ofelia would toil up cement steps to the landing outside our third-floor apartment, her tired arms full of grocery sacks, her hair stuck in wet black strands against her forehead. Inside, cockroaches skittered across the pink linoleum. Grime accumulated in every hot, damp crevice of the crowded apartment and our bodies, no matter how tenaciously she tracked it with her rags and Pine-Sol, no matter how many shallow baths we took with our melting bars of Ivory. The portable fans followed us throughout the apartment, sentries posted wherever we planned to sit or labor for more than a moment. When I think of my aunt now, I picture her always with a box fan in one hand, the cord clasped in the other, hunting an outlet.

In the hot closeness of our four rooms and bath, the highboy was a dark forest, a cool and shaded haven for the eyes. Inside it, things sparkled and glittered, crisp, different from our real life of sagging and dampness, of pink flowered sofa cushions compacted where our behinds had sat. With my forehead pushed against the highboy's glass, I peered into its alluring, wintry world the way my aunt stared at the television. For long, dreamy minutes, my mind drifting, I'd stand as though glued to the glass, mentally catapulting myself from crystalline cliffs into icy fjords. Within the crystal bowl, the very air seemed to overflow and spill like glassy liquid down its sides. It rippled with cool clarity, like nothing else in my life.

"What are you, catatonic?" my aunt once snapped.

TV was her escape, and the show she watched religiously was *Queen for a Day*, a game show that reigned in the fifties and early sixties. *Queen for a Day* selected the most woeful tales from those of the thousands of housewives who competed to sit in the live audience at the Moulin Rouge Restaurant on Sunset Boulevard. The anointed were transfigured with makeup and curlers into temporary TV aristocracy. Onstage, each of four chosen contestants told her sad story to the host, Jack Bailey, and the audience would clap for the woman they deemed most miserable. The most pitiful, according to the Applause Meter, would be draped in a red velvet robe, crowned with gems, and shown the new household appliances she'd won! She'd cry with happiness, and the audience would smile and feel good. Because it was the show's sponsor, we brushed our teeth with Pepsodent.

I hated *Queen for a Day*; it was dumb. Aunt Ofelia never talked about what happened afterwards. She never acknowledged that the woman—the winner, the queen!—would have to hand back her crown and her robe. (I wondered if they cried again.) And then she'd have to return to her life. With a new washing machine, sure, but still: *her life*—the life so terrible strangers had clapped hard for her. There she'd be, back in her flowered housedress with the kids screaming and the bills unpaid. A day only lasted so long.

My aunt Ofelia composed her narrative fervently, month after month, hoping to swap her suffering for a coronation. She would write and rewrite her story in the evening, after the dishes were washed, sitting alone at the kitchen table, reading it aloud, practicing, infusing her voice with pathos and cracks, phrasing her sacrifices sweetly, as if shaping dough, offering them to an imaginary crowd like Jesus giving loaves to the multitudes. I could hear her from my dark bed. Sometimes her voice slipped from its mournful, pleading tone into one more flat and bitter. Her terminology grew crueler, and I could hear her lighting one Old Gold cigarette after another: the scratch of the lighter's small metal wheel, her quick inhale.

I think the alchemy of telling and retelling her story made the little miseries of her days bearable, even valuable, transforming them into commodities she could store up, describe, and proffer for exchange. She was sure she'd be chosen one day, once she'd saved the money for the ticket to LA and bought the outfit she had already picked out at Montgomery Ward. Jack Bailey would surely choose her, and I was the key to her success. Raising the illegitimate daughter of her no-good, alcohol-infested slut of a baby sister, as she phrased it alone one night after too many cigarettes, was the jewel in her crown of suffering.

Once my mother died, of course, she too enjoyed a transformation of sorts. I never heard the word *whore* used about her again. In the public eulogies, she became a saint, an angel who had lost her way too young and been taken advantage of by those musicians she worshipped like gods until one beat her into a coma.

Thirteen, I was there for the unplugging. I held my wrist next to hers and realized that music wasn't the only thing that made Aunt Ofelia's lip wrinkle when she spoke of my mother's choices: my skin against hers was like cocoa against café con leche. And at thirteen, I knew what that meant. My mother had seen herself as simply Cuban, not black or white or brown. I suddenly knew why Aunt Ofelia, with her milky skin, stiffened when she took me out in public. People imagined that I was her daughter, that she was the one who'd done that, with those men.

"This is what happens," Aunt Ofelia said briskly, pinching my arm for emphasis, "when you let the boys have what they want."

I knew what she meant. My guilty secret was that I wanted it, too. I stared at the boys in my eighth-grade class like once I'd stared at the bowl. The veins on their forearms, the dip of their throats. But did letting the boys have what we both wanted mean this kind of end? The breathing tubes, the lines of black stitches on a face so young? No wonder Aunt Ofelia stayed a widow, lighting candles to her dead husband on Friday and

Saturday nights instead of going on dates like our neighbors teased her to.

There in the hospital, even with the smell of bleach and the white flickering fluorescence, my mother was still more beautiful than anyone I'd ever met. By that time, her bruises had faded, and the very curves of her face seemed made for love, as if her eyes might suddenly flutter open and gaze warmly on me. Her whole face would light with a smile. "Baby," she would say, opening her arms. "My baby. I've been looking for you." I wanted to crawl in next to her and die, too. I wanted to stroke her hair, but Aunt Ofelia pulled my hand away, so I just watched as her olive skin paled, and then we left. It was the only time I had been allowed to see her.

At eighteen still a virgin but deft with my fingers, I married the man Aunt Ofelia chose, Rudolfo Finale. Twenty-six, he had a solid job as the assistant manager of the local Winn-Dixie, and he was good-looking enough. He would be steady, my aunt Ofelia prophesied, as faithful as could be expected of any husband, and we'd get groceries at a discount.

I wasn't particularly eager to marry Rudolfo or anyone else, but my options were slenderer than the waist Aunt Ofelia pinned into draped white satin, her hands fussing around me with needles and thread while she groused. She had spoken: it was time to move out. Rudolfo was not exciting, but then life (outside the highboy) generally wasn't. School was boring, yet I graduated. Though my job as a checker at Sears was mundane, I pressed my clothes and went. Church was tedious, but I genuflected and slid in next to Aunt Ofelia every Sunday and confessed my dull misdemeanors through the screen at some father, who absolved me with minimal fuss. My prayers I said by rote, not caring much if God heard. So the idea that I should be expected to wed Rudolfo and thus put paid to my aunt's long sacrifice came as no surprise. It unfolded as mildly as if I were turning the pages of a script. More than anything, I wanted children. I wanted to hold them and teach them to talk. I wanted to listen to their soft chatter and squeeze them in my arms, and push them on the swings at the playground, and crouch at the bottom of the slide, waiting and laughing as they zoomed down at me, and sweep them up in my arms and spin in the warm sunlight, laughing and dizzy. Marriage was what you did to get that.

After the quiet, uncostly ceremony, Rudolfo installed me in a clean little cement-block bungalow in Opa-locka, seven miles from Aunt Ofelia's apartment. With a carport and metal awnings over the windows, and everything trimmed a cheerful peach, it was satisfactory. He asked me to stop working, so I did, and I kept the house immaculate. At night, Rudolfo would spit on his hand so there would not be pain.

"I hope it was good for you," he would say afterward, careful not to phrase it as a question.

"Thank you," I would always reply with a quick rub of his arm, referring to his solicitude and not the act. In this way, we were able to make four years go by.

Then it was 1969; college students were wearing short skirts and having sex, the TV said, and Viet Nam was making everyone argue. *Queen for a Day* had gone off the air five years before, only to return briefly with a new host. It wasn't the same, and my aunt—never applauded, never crowned for the long, thankless efforts of her life—had fallen into a depression. Hope had disappeared. She had come to this country with only her sister, who'd gone full-speed to the devil. She'd watched her young husband die of stomach cancer, and then shepherded me to a decent adulthood I didn't thank her for. Now her black hair was going gray, and her ankles were fat. America had never clapped for her. Lonely and bored, she called every day or two to ask what I was cooking for dinner and if I was pregnant yet. She spoke Spanish all the time now; what was the point, she said, in trying anymore? Sometimes I just let it ring.

But no children came. Rudolfo, an old-school macho, was sure it was my fault, my body's reluctance to produce what it should. He insisted that my organs be interrogated by all the latest technology. I went to the doctor's alone.

A week later, I dropped Rudolfo off at Winn-Dixie at eight o'clock in the morning and drove back to the clinic to hear the results. Waiting in the doctor's office, I sat with my white high-heeled sandals together and my matching handbag on my lap, dreading the news and what would happen next. Barren. All I wanted—the only dream that kept me going—was a child to hold. A daughter, a son. If there was no hope of that, then I would have to admit that my marriage meant nothing for me but a roof. And then what? Would I become a divorcée? What kind of life would Rudolfo's Winn-Dixie alimony buy, and who would want me again? Where would I go? I would lose my aunt, the church, all respect from the people who knew me, and I would never have a child of my own . . .

The doctor came in, sat down at his desk, opened the file, smiled up at me. His blue eyes glinted happily behind his glasses, as if he were about to share a personal success. There was nothing wrong with my fertility, he said.

When the damp rush of relief subsided back beneath my eyes and I had thanked him ten or eleven times, I felt numb, unable to think. Tottering a little, I made my way through the waiting room and outside to the parking lot and the sun's glare. Keys in my hand, I stood there. It was the middle of the day; I knew I'd left the bungalow spotless. There was no reason to return.

I got in the Barracuda and drove, turning randomly right

or left when I came to an intersection. I couldn't think. *What now? What now?* kept ringing in my head, but it wasn't a voice I recognized. My car lost itself on unfamiliar streets in the low, flat city, and I wound and twisted and doubled back, until suddenly the claustrophobic little buildings melted away, and I was shooting across a bridge, shifting into fourth gear over the sparkling water of Biscayne Bay, heading toward South Beach, where I'd never been.

The bright blue spread wide around me. Giant cruise ships were docked, waiting to bear people away to the islands, and the white cat's ears of sails jutted from distant yachts. It was thrilling to move so fast through light and air across the water, everything glittering, my foot speeding me on. The word *freedom* had always rung hollow to me before, a thing you said in school when told, but this rushing wind in my hair and the steering wheel light under my hands, I thought, must be the felt, live thing the word meant.

Once back on land, I kept driving east as far as the road went, and then turned left on a street promisingly called Ocean Drive. Cars moved slowly. Viejitas hobbled down the sidewalk in their pin-pricked beige orthopedic shoes, and handsome men sauntered alone. One beautiful run-down old hotel after another slid by on my left as the car rolled north. When I found a parking space, I got out and walked quickly across the green sward of grass and coconut palms and sea-grape trees to the dunes. And then, the heels of my little white sandals sinking into the sand as I struggled up, I was cresting the top of the dune, I was over, and then I was on the beach, with nothing between me and the blue Atlantic. I took my sandals off. They dangled from my fingers as I walked toward the water, thinking.

Rudolfo would not welcome the news of my results. Him, sterile? There would be yelling, the fist against kitchen cupboards. I wandered through the scattered sunbathers until I found a rounded hollow in the sand that would hold me, and I sat. Around me were other girls my age, but they lay stretched and oiled in black bikinis, sunning their flesh. Under its neat blue shirtwaist, my twenty-two-year-old body was as smooth and young as theirs were. Girls knocked a volleyball over a net, and browned men with shoulder-length curls and flat bellies loped down the beach in surfing shorts, laughing. I wondered if they spat on their hands or if they knew something different.

A bottled coconut scent floated over from the sunbathers, mixing with the ocean's smell of salt. It reminded me of the shore at Matheson Hammock, where Aunt Ofelia had taken me to play a few times when I was younger. There, the line of the man-made atoll with its string of palms blocked the view of the ocean. The waters were placid, protected—ideal for families. My aunt chose it for that reason, she said: it was safe.

South Beach was different. I flexed my feet into the warm sand. I couldn't believe I'd lived for twenty-two years in Miami and never seen the unbroken blue line of the horizon, never felt this fresh salt wind.

"Complainers end up with nothing at all." I could hear my aunt's chiding voice in my head. "Thank the Lord for what you've got."

But what did I have?

Because it was October and cooling off for the season, I had not yet begun to sweat, but the sun's heat pressed me down, and the sand cupped me in its warmth. I slid my toes down into its sliding grains, tucked my handbag next to me, and lay back. The sun heated my face, my closed eyelids, and the hands I folded neatly over my waist. To my left and then my right, repeating in a loud and steady rhythm, the surf rushed in, breaking, like the blood in your own ears. Waves throbbed, crashing and frothing, blotting out every sound but the occasional shrill bicker of the gulls or an exultant cry from the volleyball court. Though my skin was warm, I felt myself falling into a cool, dark trance, the way as a child I'd fallen into the sparkling scenes in the crystal bowl. I lay in the cradling sand, not thinking, my mind an open, dark blank. Long minutes swept by, marked only by the shush of the waves and the cries of gulls. My body loosened against the sand. I seemed to be floating. I felt like a child.

Odd, fragmented visions began to swirl in my mind's eye, shimmering up from the darkness. A vast bed, its white linens rumpled, and the sun of late afternoon spilling across it. The row of hotels I'd rolled past, their right angles smoothed into curves, looking like they fell out of history: the Colony, the Boulevard, the Starlite, the Tides. Then dark smoke swallowed them, and I could see, illuminated in strangely extravagant detail, the terrace of the Rumba Palace, a restaurant I'd glanced at driving by, and me, sitting alone at a table, hot wind in my hair, my body languid with release, eating my dollar bowl of black beans ladled over arroz amarillo, sipping a mojito, the green folds of its spearmint leaves swiveling amid the ice like seaweed in an undersea garden. And for dessert, platanos fritos, crisped hot and sweet. Then that, too, dissolved, and, like household appliances lined up before me, I saw an assortment of men, all carefully selected for their resemblance to a younger, tauter, tanned version of Rudolfo, a Rudolfo who laughed and cared what I thought. And I saw myself sitting across my own living room from the real Rudolfo, explaining with feigned embarrassment that yes, the problem lay with me, my defective body, and that I would have to go into the clinic every week for fertility treatments so I could conceive his child. His gruff nod. I saw babies in my arms, baby after baby, as many babies as I wanted, all the color of me. And then the dark cloud sank across my vision again, and I lay limp in the warm bowl of the sand for long, abandoned minutes, mindlessly breathing.

When at last I sat up, looking around and raking the grains of sand from my hair with slow strokes, it seemed that all the things around me had fallen into a pattern: the quiet turning of people's bodies on their towels seemed synchronized with the rippling flights of the gulls rising, swooping over the water in a wide loop, and returning as one to the sand, and the chattery-quick steps of the sand-colored terns, darting toward the receding surf, pecking, and darting quickly upshore when the next wave broke. Everything was part of a rhythm.

I rose with fresh energy, my sandals in my hand, sand falling from my dress. The keys to the Barracuda were in my handbag. The MacArthur Causeway was a bridge I could cross and recross.

Along the waterline jogged a beautiful man, flashing his white smile. His eyes—like Rudolfo's, only happy—lingered on mine, and I smiled and dipped my chin, just once, just slightly, and his pace dropped to a walk. He veered from the water and toward me; he was approaching. I glanced down as he drew closer, my pulse beating violently in my throat, the salt air quickening between my lips. It would be this easy. A future of secret pleasures crystallized before me.

But I turned, suddenly frightened, and walked rapidly away, heading back up toward the dunes. It was all too much, too fast.

"Hey," the man called, like a question behind me, but I kept walking, the sand giving way under my bare feet. Maybe I would give Aunt Ofelia a call, just to say hi; I'd seen phone booths on Ocean Drive.

Nearby, one tern had nested into a small dip in the sand. Her soft dun feathers blended into the tan that surrounded her. Only her bright eye shone dark as she glanced around.

The Pottery Barn and the Foster Child

My husband and I are hardly the types to take in children for the money, much less keep them in cages and do vile things to them. I know what foster parents can be; I read the papers. But we didn't need the money, and we weren't closet sadists. We just wanted a child.

We're not the types, either, to jet off to Russia or China or Guatemala, when all the fertility options fail to work, like more and more couples do, including several of our acquaintances. The women seem the most proprietary—especially those single middle-aged professional women with their little girls from China—and all of them think everyone's so fascinated with their saga of getting the child in Siberia or Viet Nam or wherever: how they got sick over there from the water, or how they scrutinized the videotapes from the orphanage for signs of delayed development, or how the baby wouldn't stop crying the whole plane ride home but it was so, so worth it.

Accessory babies, I call them. Not to my friends' faces, of course. All those little black-haired, shiny-eyed girls and towhead boys being toted about like one more luxury object, just a grand legitimizing excuse for parading around the Eddie Bauer strollers with wheelbrakes and a one-pedal release, the titanium Jeep strollers, the aubergine Bugaboo Frog strollers, the Vuitton diaper bags, the pink and orange Oilily baby cardigans, the dear little Clayeux rompers, the BabyBjörn carriers strapped around the mother's unaltered figure. Charming: the parents' comfortable means and open minds perpetually on display, the private pain of their infertility transformed to a public performance of their wealth and international brotherhood.

I wouldn't call myself opinionated, but others have. Prickly, critical, rigorous, judgmental. A bitch—which is okay. It fits. I like to win, and I like to be right. The law was an easy choice for me.

Though rare, there exist adoptive parents who try. They move to neighborhoods full of their child's ethnic group, where they themselves become suddenly minorities. They choose open adoptions and remain in touch, even bringing the mother to visit; they take family vacations in the child's home country each year. They learn the child's home language and speak it, however imperfectly, so that original music doesn't wither in him.

But I was forty-two. I wanted to have a child, not overhaul my life, however virtuously. And I couldn't subject a brown child to a lifetime of stares and curiosity, of being a perpetual minority of one, an exotic display. I couldn't let myself imagine, as our friends did, that our mere love could compensate for the daily experience of questions in everyone's eyes. The habits of mind formed in childhood (I knew) were hard to break, so our child's legacy would be a lifetime of unease. And I wouldn't be able to counter that. I'm not a warm person. In those moments, my husband and I would be just two white middle-class, middle-aged lawyers, skeptically questioning for details, imagining the testimony of the opposition, as is our habit, and our child would know herself to be hopelessly alone.

When we talked to the foster care office and learned there are kids who need families right here, Brian and I sent the baby money we'd saved to an orphanage in Uganda, for the children most Americans would not, could not want: the too old, too black, too damaged, or insufficiently cute. We decided instead to take in a local foster child and work toward adoption.

"Oh, but that's so *difficult*," my women friends cooed, their groomed eyebrows raised in what was supposed to look like admiration and concern for me—but was in fact, I knew, their own self-exculpation. Those children are too damaged, unstable, they said. Had I heard the story about the eight-year-old foster boy who slit his new parents' throats one night? "You're playing with fire," they said. And even if the kid does turn out to be okay, the arrangement isn't permanent. You risk getting all attached and then having them be taken back by the courts.

My thought, which I tried to express mildly, is that if damaged, unstable six-year-olds and thirteen-year-olds are required to take that risk, then I—as an educated, successful, and stable adult—am probably capable and probably should.

Besides, I knew my friends' worries were bullshit; it was just a class thing. My friend Amanda, who bought a baby in Siberia last year, once moaned to me about going to watch her husband's city-league softball games because of the other wives in the bleachers.

"Not to be a snob or anything," she said. "But they're, like, *factory* women. I don't know how to start a conversation with them. So they're all chatting away, and I'm sitting there thinking, Jesus Christ, Jeremy, just strike out already." She spread her pretty hands in the air over our lattes, replaying her exasperation, shaking her head. "And, oh my god, Kate, you should see their *toenails*."

Apparently, Brian and I are not the typical applicants for a foster child. The social worker's face relaxed in relief when I opened the door, though surely our neighborhood had already tipped her off that we weren't going to be the sketchy sort. I toured her through: tiled kitchen, good art, brimming bookshelves,

French doors, new electronics, a gunite pool we rarely use. A lovely gender-neutral child's bedroom with its own bath, the shower curtain swimming with bright fish. Two attorneys, happily married, and everything kept spotless by a weekly housekeeper. Hiking vacations in Europe and Peru.

The paperwork was a formality.

We'd both reduced our hours already. I wasn't willing to stay home with the child, so we'd want school-age; I'd pick it up from school each day, and both Brian and I would be home for dinner and on weekends.

The social worker couldn't have been happier, she said, to accommodate our needs.

And here sits the object of our desires, a girl-child torpid and unlovely. Tina. She is everything I wanted, which is to say: not a status object, not adorable, not just the thing to complete my age-appropriate ensemble. Rather, a child in genuine need.

But the drab fact of her depresses me. A good washing and conditioning did not make her blond hair shine. It's been five weeks, and three daily meals of healthy food have not brightened her complexion. She's twelve, and lumpy-bodied, and the round cigarette scars stagger up her forearms like clichés. The parents were addicts and dealers; they occasionally loaned her out to customers as a little lagniappe. At school last fall, she tried to burn her social studies teacher with a lighter—shoved it up into her face—and that's what finally got Child Protective Services out to the house.

Now she sits on our sofa, a sullen, opaque lump of hurt, leafing through the Pottery Barn catalogue.

Tina barely talks, doesn't look at us at dinner. I drive fifty minutes each way, twice a day, so she can keep going to the same school, so that at least one thing from her life will not change unless she wants it to, and she doesn't. (They transferred her to a different social studies class.) On the ride, she stares out the window, silent. When I speak, she agrees or says nothing. Even when I invite her to choose the radio station, her eyes never leave the green blur outside.

"Don't know any," she says.

She's no trouble. She does her schoolwork without being told, sitting at the kitchen table each afternoon with the brioche and cocoa I give her. She knows how to make them last. Only after all the books are closed does she pinch up the final crumb and take her last sip, the sweet dark dregs gone cold. Twice a week she sees a therapist: on Mondays, the state-funded one, and on Thursdays, the one we pay for, the best in the city. She's "receptive," the expensive therapist tells us, not "resistant," so presumably she talks in there.

At Whole Foods this morning, after I'd dropped Tina off, I saw a woman my age with her little Chinese baby in a Snugli. Obviously besotted, the woman wrapped her arms around the child, jiggled it, squeezed it, and the baby grinned a toothless grin. She brushed her hand softly across its cheek, across its black thick hair. I had to grip the handle of my cart and look away.

Tina prefers not to be touched, not even in the most innocuous of ways: a pat on the shoulder, a comradely ruffle of the hair. She shrinks from our hands. Even this, she accomplishes as inconspicuously as possible, as if she doesn't want to risk angering or insulting us by her withdrawal.

We agreed not to take it personally. I wouldn't want anyone touching me, either—especially not adults, and especially not parents, and especially not new fake parents.

At first, her real parents gazed out from a frame on her nightstand. Their wasted stares and loose grins chilled me. Theirs are the kinds of faces I help prosecute. But the social worker said that it was a good idea, that we should let her keep any transitional objects she wanted. One day—week three, I think it was—I went into Tina's room with a folded stack of laundry, and the picture was gone. I put the laundry away and peeked out the window. She was sitting by the pool, staring down at the Pottery Barn catalogue on her lap. I slid the nightstand drawer open, and there was the photograph, face down.

I'm not sure why she's so mesmerized by the Pottery Barn catalogue, of all the books and magazines we have. She'll sit for an hour, eyes dreamy, placidly paging through it. It's like a tranquilizer for an already tranquilized animal. I confess that I'm a little disappointed: it's a bland, banal choice, and I'd hoped for a sharper edge, a more critical or at least rebellious sensibility, given where she's come from. I'd allowed myself to hope for *interesting*, if nothing else. This was a girl who'd shoved a lighter in her teacher's face; surely she'd have more life. But I supposed it was perfectly natural, perfectly American: to want what you've been told to want, what has been kept from you.

I wondered exactly why its slick pages fascinated her, what soothing escapism it offered. Did she insert an imagined self into those quiet, unpeopled rooms? Did she wrap herself in long velvet drapes, smooth and invisible, or lean on the down-wrapped arm of a sofa? Perhaps it seemed simply a book of possibilities, full of comfort and peace, a hundred rooms unlike rooms she'd known.

Tina. Even her name tinkles cheaply, a title for a trinket. At lunches and teas lately, I keep being introduced to all these smooth-cheeked East Asian girl babies named Emma, Audrey, Hamilton, or Rose, or to little Nicaraguan toddlers named Thomas or Charles.

"Huh," I say pleasantly, that noncommittal, socially useful sound, and devote myself to wondering what their names would have been if those hundreds of thousands of American dollars had been funneled directly to the birthmothers. When all the sex and the shots in my ass failed, and it became painfully clear that adoption was our only choice, I read books about what it does to babies not to bond, or to be taken from their mothers once they've bonded. I've listened to my friends confess their embarrassed relief that these particular third-world birthmothers will never be able to afford to come looking. Not across oceans.

Tina's parents have made no attempts at contact, though they live right here in our county, though the social worker encouraged us to let her talk to them whenever she wanted.

I took Tina shopping soon after she moved in, to personalize her room. A twelve-year-old girl, a credit card, and me, overly eager to make her feel welcome. Two of my older friends had daughters Tina's age, and they warned me to brace myself for financial ruin. They laughed, shrugging, as they told stories of their daughters' exorbitant requests, their own acquiescence. Chuckling indulgently, they were strangely specific as they detailed brand names and costs, and I couldn't help wondering if this was just an advanced version of Bugaboo Frog.

"Huh," I said.

But Tina wanted nothing.

"No," she'd say, listless, and then remember to add, "thank you"—her delay not insolent, just absent. She had everything she needed, she claimed, and it was true: we had frantically stocked the gender-neutral, impersonal child's room with every necessity as soon as we got the social worker's call. So the beige slate stayed blank. I ended up buying her a couple of pairs of jeans—not even expensive jeans, or inappropriate-for-a-girl-her-age jeans, which in itself was a little depressing: she didn't try to wrangle anything out of me that I didn't want to give.

I'd stocked the bookshelf with YA titles recommended by the Barnes & Noble salesgirl. I'd fanned out teen girl magazines on the little desk. And there they stayed. The Pottery Barn catalogue was the only printed material she'd pick up.

Brian and I had bought a couple of Pottery Barn rugs years ago—one for the guest room, one for my office—and the catalogues just kept coming. On the day Tina arrived, a fresh one was stacked with the mail. Now she takes it everywhere: poolside, to bed, into the bathroom. It's tattered like an old stuffed toy. When she's not doing homework or eating a meal with us, she lives in a Pottery Barn trance. A+ in consumerism.

She's on our sofa now, looking through it again, arms held stiffly to her sides, feet together on the floor, still not at home enough here to curl up or sprawl, though we've assured her that socks on the furniture are perfectly okay. Brian will be home in a couple of hours. For now, it's just the two of us. Wide washes of afternoon light fall from the clerestory windows.

It makes an odd tableau. With its mix of good furniture and really fine furniture, of framed black-and-white photos of Brian and me laughing in the places we've been, art objects poised on their shelves, our living room could, itself, be a spread in a catalogue. Except for Tina, the blot on the image. A plain little thing, trapped in that awkward age girls go through, made infinitely duller and uglier by the things she carries.

I move across the sunlit room and lower myself onto the cushion next to her, carefully placing a few inches of upholstery between us, expecting her to shrink away. But she slowly turns the page. It's as if I'm not there. I can hear her breathe.

It takes an effort to keep the false cheer from my voice. *Dear God, let me not sound perky.* I shoot for quiet, unobtrusive, the thing she's trying so hard to be. I fold my hands in my lap and watch. I hope that when I do think of something to say, my tone will come out casual, nonchalant.

My hair's blond, too.

I went through an awkward age.

"So what stuff do you like?" I ask.

For a moment, she doesn't speak, and I think she's going to ignore me. It occurs to me that, in other circumstances, we could be a real mother and daughter, engaged in the ritual of poring over consumer goods, comparing our choices as a form of entertainment, communion.

She clears her throat. "This," she finally says. Her nail-bitten finger slides across the page to pause on a sprig of white coral on a shelf. "This." A glass bowl full of dried sea urchins. Photos of laughing children tacked crookedly to a bulletin board. Through a window, a leafy oak.

The pages slowly turn. A vase of red-edged tulips, all blown open on a sunny ledge. A golden retriever sprawled next to his dish. A black-and-white shot of a couple hugging. Stacked river stones. A fat pot of rosemary.

None of the things she fingers has an item number. They're all things added by a team of paid stylists to make the staged rooms look like real life happens there.

Her finger keeps slowly gliding, pausing, gliding on, tracing her desire across the pages. A loaf of fresh-baked bread on a kitchen counter, three slices cut and fanned out, the knife sprinkled with brown crumbs.

The last page turns, and her finger skids to a stop: in the fireplace, a fire. Her hands go still. She doesn't move or look at me.

"They're not for sale," she says, her voice flat.

My pulse beats in my eardrums. Sunlight blurs everything.

"I'll get them for you," I whisper.

The Cave

From childhood, Holly loved fierce, dark tastes: licorice, black-
strap molasses, creamed coffee left unsweetened. They were mysterious and rich, powerful, like sex must be, she thought later:
like real love and sex must be, after one has gotten past the trap-
pings of red panties and garter belts and on into the rich dark
swim of real sex, the warmth and odor of the cave.

She had grown up in Brazil, in a fantasyland of maids and
luxury apartments and her father's white wealth, her mother's
brittle beauty. What lay outside that tight, well-guarded sphere
was still a fantasyland, one of costumes and feathered masks and
men dancing drunk in the streets, the brown globes of women's
asses glossy with oil. All of it was rotten, she had sensed since a
very young child, fascinating but rotten, the white and brown
worlds equally thrilling and desperate and false, the whip of the
Carnival street dance as dangerous as the glass-topped tables her
mother favored, their corners protruding, the whole apartment
a fragile, rigid maze, as dangerous as the diamond eardrops that
meant they'd be gone all night again.

Alone in her room, Holly read *The Secret Garden* and longed
not for a rich uncle or a mansion, or even a walled forgotten
garden she could bring back to life, but for Martha, the Cock-
ney maid, someone who would be there and be patient and
tell her the truth. Air-conditioned and glassed in, she chewed
her licorice and stared down at the dancers and torches whirl-

ing seven stories below. She wondered how the licorice felt, its brown warmth glistening in the dark soft cave of her mouth, its body mauled by her teeth, its juices loosed by the squeezing muscle of her tongue. Could licorice possibly be *sentient*? Her father, tall and slender and balding, with a stoop that not even the glamour of a tuxedo could improve, would sit on the edge of her bed at night and quiz her on the English vocabulary words she'd learned at the international school. He'd add two or three of his own. *Ineffable. Transcendental. Ekphrasis.* Or when her mother was in the room, *placate, ameliorate, prevaricate.* Holly learned others, too, just by listening. Multinational. Pharmaceutical. On the pages of her father's memo pads, embossed with his name and a little design, she wrote and illustrated stories: iguanas in cufflinks and ball gowns, dancing, with tiny martini glasses gripped in their claws. She stapled the sheets together and read them aloud to her dolls and animals, then solemnly stacked them in neat rows on her bookshelf. She felt sure she would be a writer one day.

It hadn't happened. At seventeen, she'd been shipped to her mother's alma mater, Bryn Mawr, where she'd *indulged* herself— her mother's words—in two nervous breakdowns and one serious, ambitious, and very nearly successful attempt at death. (A few hundred miles from Bryn Mawr, Holly would learn later, at an equally prestigious girls' college, another bright young woman was similarly indulging herself and would soon become phenomenally famous. Who knew? Later, she would succeed. It was the glasses of milk and the sandwiches, neat on the bedside table, the cloth rolled under the door where the children slept, that made Holly cry when she learned of it. She gave thanks that Mario, who was thank god no genius and, essentially, a good man, had left her standing. A genius, she knew, could have destroyed her. It was a relief. Her child would never sleepily eat a sandwich while her own body lay in the next room like a nightmare.)

"I think it's the snow," she wrote to her parents from her bed in the expensive sanitarium. "And the way the birds here are all gray or brown. And so small. So dull and desperate for any little crumb. It's cold. I don't want to come home, though." Neither of her parents replied; they were divorcing, so there was no home left in Brazil for her anyway. Her mother moved to San Francisco and her father was sent to Toronto by his company. On the morning of her graduation, when her friends wore caps and gowns—and, if they were lucky, engagement rings—she sat in a diner eating pancakes with Mario, thirty-six, her boyfriend, a Chicano labor organizer. She'd asked that her diploma be mailed to her apartment, but when it arrived, she was already gone.

Spanish was close to Portuguese, and Holly lipped her way easily into Mario's circle, into the community, the movement. The workers knew she was rich, a pretty joke to be tolerated, with her green eyes and milky skin and pale gold hair, and she lived in the tents and picked until her pale hands bled and callused. There was a dreamy softness in her face that made some of the women hate her, a dreaminess that thrives only in leisure and safety, that had been crushed out of their own childhoods at a bitterly young age. But Mario protected her from them. He married her, and together they had a daughter, lived in tents and shelters all over the country, cashed Holly's checks and donated them to the effort. They split up fondly, sadly, reluctantly, when the third pretty young Chicana sat up startled with Mario in their bed one afternoon and Holly knew, suddenly and finally, that despite his apologies and promises it would never end.

She took Helena and went to Chicago for graduate school.

Bed with Mario, she acknowledged to herself in the quiet of her new apartment, had not been what she'd dreamed of as a girl, through there had been hunger and excitement. Mario's copy of *The Joy of Sex* and a book on tantrism had lain next to their sleeping roll. She had been pretty and eager, and her hair had hung around her like a gold shining curtain when she arched over Mario in the candlelight, like a painting, its borders shimmering with hammered gold leaf. Ineffable, transcendent. She had felt that, at times, or tried to, or come close. But words had always been there; there had been no obliteration, no darkness, no silent union of the senses, which she'd begun craving when the first bites of licorice had dissolved in her mouth long ago. Mario had loved her. He hadn't treated her like a white-girl trophy, hadn't talked down to her about politics, hadn't made her walk around in high heels naked for him like a private peep show. He'd given her the best of himself, she knew, despite the other girls. Together they'd eaten their cardamom seeds and counted their breaths, and she'd had orgasm after orgasm. But her mind had never shut up.

We'd made a wrong turn, the human race had, Holly was convinced. She read articles about gorillas, watched documentaries about them. Animals were simple. They didn't build things; they didn't pretend not to feel what they felt; they carried their children around and held them in their arms. At some ancient moment, Holly believed, there had been a choice. Some ape had looked at simple honest vulnerable love, body love, the known comforts of fur and licking, and then dreamed instead a dream of cities and wealth, complexity and lies and power. And here we are, she thought. Here's Chicago. Here's nursery school, strangers paid to hold Helena, and the El and a master's degree when what I'd love is to throw my life down in front of Louis Leakey like his three maidens and say, "Which primate do you want me to study? Send me to the forest of your choosing," which was not quite practical given her sole responsibility—Mario was somewhere between Tucson and Seattle—for a two-year-old.

After Holly finished her second degree, she wrote to her father, asking for an inordinate sum of money "to complete my education." The check came, the amount exact; at least he read her letters. With everything they needed squeezed and squashed into a backpack, Holly and Helena flew to New York and, in a 747 with a spiral staircase to a glassy lounge where they pointed at stars together, to Paris. She hired a car to Lascaux and paid an exorbitant amount to be taken, just the two of them, into the caves by a guide holding only a torch. "No flashlights," her letter had requested, and she'd waited until she'd heard back before booking their flight.

In the cool dark of the cave, the canteen slung over her shoulder and Helena clasped at her hip, she gazed at aurochs and bison and cave lions whose muscles rippled in the wavering light, at horses whose legs seemed to gallop in the flame's flicker. This is the way they must have seen it, then, when they painted it. "Please," she murmured to the guide, who had launched into his programmed spiel, "you don't have to say anything."

She looked down at Helena in her arms, the child's eyes huge, her mouth a ripe little rose. What was Helena thinking? What did she see? She was a soft firm warmth in Holly's arms, a weight like an anchor, a core like the earth's hot center. No one could know what Holly felt for this small animal, this cub. The cave was silent. Standing there in the dampness and thin wind, Holly knew that this was the pivot point, the fulcrum of her life. She knew, too, that being aware of it while it was happening was a rare gift, and it made her heart beat fast. The child in her arms *was* the cave, the mystery of flesh from flesh, the deep complete attunement to the animal beat of another. Primitive. Profound.

If the guide had been a different sort of man, she might have liked to take the torch from his hands and wedge it in a crevice of the rock, and set Helena in a safe dry spot to watch the animals like watching a Saturday-morning cartoon, and fuck him freely on the stone floor. But he was only the sort of man he was, so she just smiled to herself in the half-light. And maybe that was the mistake she'd been making: to look for that warmth with a man. The cave said no. The cave said: *This child.*

Three months later the two of them landed in Quito, and Holly fell in love. She fell in love with the city, its low white buildings unfurled across a basin high in the mountains, its silver Mary's arms embracing all. She loved the placid way people pulled out decks of cards when the city's frequent power outages made the subway halt. She loved the way people took to Helena, whose shining brown curls and perfect baby Spanish made her seem like one of their own, and the way Helena was completely safe with the housekeeper's family when Holly's work took her into the mountains. In the villages, where the air was thin and little would grow, she was the first white woman and the first nutrition worker most people had seen. The vegetation was too sparse for goats or pigs, and without protein, the children grew slowly and stayed small. Sometimes hiking up the dirt track, with manuals in her satchel, Holly felt an expansion in the center of her forehead as if the cool thin air were rushing directly into her brain. All was huge and silent, a spaciousness unlike any she'd known before. Then she'd arrive in the village, and the warm chatter and excitement and work would drive the silence from her mind. Falling asleep, she would remember it, and think, *This must be my life's purpose. I am doing good. I am working hard and honestly without thought of self,* and she would sleep well.

Down in the city, she made friends with her neighbors, planted herbs in pots on the terrace of the little house, and showed Helena how to pick them, how to knot thread around the stems and hang them upside down from hooks she'd twisted into the kitchen shelf. She taught her how to sound out letters in the big comic-book primers she had ordered from New York. They sat on the steps, tracing their fingers over the letters. "C, cat," Holly crooned, her nose in her daughter's dark hair.

"Gato," Helena corrected, giggling.

Years passed. Helena went to a local school, the villagers' children were growing taller than they ever had before, and Holly, with her US education, her bona fide good works, her blond hair bobbed now and her eyes unearthly green against her gold skin, had become a favorite in a circle of wealthy liberals, where she met Ramon Paredes, son of an oil executive. Handsome, shy, and twelve years her senior, Ramon didn't rush. On their seventh date, he led her into his room, sat down on the floor facing her, and took her hands in his. She was startled. The dusk was quiet and dim, and the room was large but simple: a bare floor, a single bed, a brown blanket, tall windows that looked out over the darkening city. She noticed that his breaths were matching hers. The room got darker. Soon she could see only the small bent squares of light on his eyes. In her belly she felt a warm stirring, and then a pulse, and then a stillness, like an animal had been roused from sleep and was alert, waiting. When he leaned slowly toward her and kissed her lightly, slowly, she felt each soft segment of his lips as they pressed and slid on hers. There was time, he seemed to be saying. There was infinite time. There was only the darkness, their bodies, the ecstatic end of thinking. It was simple, silent, holy. Words stopped. A dark flood swept everything away.

They married, against the predictable social fuss his family was obliged to make: she was an Anglo, a foreigner; she was divorced, she had another man's child. But at heart, they liked her, and she and Helena moved into Ramon's immense apartment in the compound of buildings and gardens his father owned, and Ramon bought a bigger bed. They ate dinner with the extended family in a vast dining hall with heavy dark furniture too big and stiff for comfort, but they ate their breakfasts in Ramon's bed—Helena would follow the maid and tray in—and their lunch in the little kitchen, sandwiches Holly made herself, slicing avocados and singing in the quiet light. It did seem as though all the pieces had come together. *This may be*, she dared to think, *my reward.* The new housekeeper was almost as good with Helena as the old one had been, and Helena was more independent now anyway, nine years old. Holly's stays in the mountain villages could stretch a little—two weeks, three—and when she returned, Ramon would be there, and chilled wine and the big bed, and they'd spend a whole day and night together before emerging. The room, the bed, seemed like a temple, a mosque, somewhere sacred, like a place she had to go to consecrate herself when she came back to the city. The maid would knock and leave trays of food outside the door and go silently away.

Work and love. And recognition, which trickled into Holly's life as a surprise and then grew: certificates and plaques and dinners in her honor, handshakes from the mayor for her work with indigenous people, grants from foundations in the States. Everything seemed to be going well for them; all their problems melted easily away. When Helena, eleven, started faltering academically and seemed unhappy, their friends put in a word at Quito's most exclusive private school, and after a few months as a day student, Helena said she wanted to board there. The family was relieved; she had been getting a little difficult, a little petulant. She seemed happier there.

And when one morning Holly rolled quickly from the bed, her hand over her mouth, and rushed to the bathroom, she felt inhabited by utter joy. Another baby, another piece of magic, another love to overwhelm her, shatter her. She stood there on the tile, remembering Helena and the cave. She held her flat belly, swayed side to side, humming, her eyes closed. And this baby—the thought stole guiltily into her mind—this baby came from a more complete, perfect love. What would such a child be like, with Ramon's beauty and hers, the fruit of their perfect lovemaking? Holly felt the quake of hubris, but the question was irresistible; besides, everyone else would ask it anyway—the beauty part—when she and Ramon made the announcement. It was only a natural thing to wonder.

And when the baby was born, he was indeed exquisite, placid and pretty and adored by everyone, even Helena, who came home at holidays. Perfect, perfect.

So it came as a surprise, two years later, when Helena was expelled from the very school to which Holly had spared no expense to send her. When the call came from the headmistress, whom Holly had thought unflappable, the woman's tone sounded genuinely appalled. Helena had been discovered in the gymnasium storage room after curfew, on the tumbling mats. With three young men.

"Street boys," the headmistress clarified. She cleared her throat. "Black boys." Her dry voice grew dryer. "Tumbling, one might say." Holly couldn't tell if it was their streetness or their blackness or their threeness that so appalled the headmistress.

"Thank you," Holly said. What was there to say? "Please send her home."

"Oh, we will," the headmistress replied. "Most certainly."

And when Helena had erupted into the dining room that evening in the middle of a brown-out, and Ramon and Ramon's parents and sister and new brother-in-law had looked up, and Holly had started to her feet, her arms opening out toward her daughter, Helena had thrown her backpack on the floor and herself into a chair. And when she'd said in English, "It was just fucking, Mom," her eyes flat and hard, when the baby had banged his spoon and cried, "Nena, Nena," holding out his arms to his sister, who ignored him and helped herself to a tortilla, rolling it and tucking it in the corner of her mouth like a cigar—when Helena turned to the rest of the family and said, in a consummately casual tone, "By the way, I'm pregnant"—Holly was as lost as she had ever been.

The Dream of the Father

Angela Cardenas was not only a liar and a bitch but also a boyfriend-stealer, which didn't keep me from being best friends with her the last three years of high school. I'm not sure what that says about me, considering even my own boyfriends weren't off-limits.

For instance like the time she and Rick Piscatelli made out in my driveway after my seventeenth birthday party while I busted ass inside, scrambling to collect all the bottles before my folks got home from the Steelers game. I didn't even know about it for almost a week until Tanya Rodebecker told me, in this surprised way like she thought for *sure* me and Rick must've broken up. But Tanya was like that, acting like she didn't mean anything; Angela would just rob you blind. Which in a way, you had to respect.

I mean, you couldn't blame her, at least I couldn't, what with me being the original wallflower of the universe. I figured she couldn't help herself, and neither could the guys, with her looking like she did. She was so pretty you couldn't even envy her, she was in such a different league. When a certain black-haired, pouty-lipped, big-bosomed actress made it big, about the time me and Angie were seniors, people started coming up to her all the time: "Has anybody ever told you that you look just like so-and-so?"

"No—really?" she'd say, all sweet and surprised-like, sucking it in like honey, although I swear I must have seen it happen at least thirty times at the mall or up at Colassessano's. If you've ever hung out with a truly beautiful girl then you know how it is, how you're not really even jealous. You just drink up the excitement of it, proud to be standing next to her. I mean maybe I wouldn't have handled it so well if she hadn't been so great. Not that she really was so great, at least if you look at it in a surface kind of way. It was more complicated than that, and I've always been enticed by complications.

Being the less pretty one, I always played the straight man when we hung around in public together, and she was the one laughing and bouncing from lap to lap, squeezing biceps, me saying, *Come on, Angie, we're gonna be late.* I remember her writing me notes in chemistry class about how it was like swallowing six raw eggs one after the other until you think you're going to throw up or die and not to start up unless I was into total gaggery because once they'd had it they wouldn't quit asking. And me taking the notes and copying the equations that pulled us through exams.

I know this is making me sound like a fool, but if you've ever been there, then you know that there are times you don't mind being taken for one. I guess I was suffering Angela to teach me something. And I learned real well, even the details, sneaking into the basement girls' room with her during lunch hour to puke our cafeteria meals into the toilets, her having to keep her weight down for cheerleading and me along for the ride. *Shit, sweetie, you got some in your hair*, she'd say. *This apple crumble shit's a bitch.*

She could eat a half-gallon of ice cream at a sitting, something I could never do, and then rush to the bathroom, a smooth chocolate gush swirling into the toilet bowl. She'd go through three half-gallons in an evening—her mom worked nightshift at McCrory's so I'd go over there and we'd watch comedies on the VCR until we were too tired to see. *Put the blusher across your nose a little bit too, honey*, she'd say in the bathroom the next morning. *It looks more natural if you glow all over.*

I never heard anybody call her a slut, exactly, but she did have a certain kind of reputation, and I guess you could say it was earned. I remember driving her car back from Kennywood Park, two hours south to home, me and Tommy Larsen in the front seat talking about him opening up his own shop someday—which he did: Larsen's Auto Body—but that was years after. And Angela with her twenty-nine-year-old in the backseat (him with an ex-wife and little girl payments) screwing all the way down I-79.

So, how much capital would you need? I ask Tommy, because my dad says stuff like that on the phone all the time. They're real quiet but her knee or something keeps pushing on the back of the seat.

Probably around five thousand to start, he says, and I say I think that's a real fine idea, because Tommy after all knows his stuff and he's a real nice guy and patient too. The twenty-nine-year-old does something that sounds like clearing his throat and the pushing stops.

He was just one of a whole bunch during the three years me and Angie were friends—older ones, married ones, even our own East Fairmont assistant football coach—but in private she was a real nice girl and would talk seriously about things, like what she wanted to do and how scared she got sometimes thinking about nuclear war and stuff like that. Sometimes we'd drive around for hours in her little car listening to the Police and not saying anything. And she wasn't a dumb girl at all.

It's taken me a lot of years of not seeing her to wonder why somebody who was secretly smart and had dreams for herself would go to such lengths to hide that away from everybody. Why she would take me so serious in private, like we were the best friends in the world, but treat me so bad when it suited her. Making out with my boyfriends and such. We talked about a lot of things, me and Angie, but there are things I still wonder about when I think of her. And it's a true story that her dad shot himself on her bed when she was twelve years old, before I knew her, but she wouldn't talk about him to save her life.

If a dead man's face can really look out of an upper-story window, if a dead man's elbow can prop itself on the sill and his shoulder can wedge against the casement. If a dead man can light a cigarette and throw the match down into the street. If a dead man's match can land in the street where his daughter waits, if it can land at the feet of his living daughter, his daughter who is alive and asleep watching the match burn at her feet. If she can see the way his eyes drink in the orange pinpoints when he pulls on the cigarette. If she can see him seeing her in the darkness. The way his eyes suck the light out of the air and swallow it, the way when she looks at his eyes she is shrinking, she feels the shrinking of her body into a tiny flicker, how she starts to float, billowing toward him across the warm dark air. If she can see him seeing her in the darkness. If he can see her in the darkness, see her in her bed with the covers pulled around. If he can see her no matter which way she moves, if he can see her in the light. If he can see her during the day, during cheerleading practice during those times when suddenly her smile muscles grow rigid and her eyes stare back, her teeth bared in a rictus grin. And Mrs. McManus yells at her to get with the other girls! and she does, she gets with the other girls, she matches her movements to theirs, her arms to their flashing arms, her legs to their leaps, her chant to their pumping voices go boys go.

Ruthless

The house was quiet, the girls at school. Clear morning light spilled through the kitchen. I stood at the sink with my hands in soapy water, looking through the window at the backyard but seeing only Liz's dark eyes and laughing, bitter mouth. I needed her.

We'd become friends twenty-two years ago, over a laundry basket spilled on the stairs of the apartment complex. I was nineteen, a year older, and she was tough, smart, a contradiction in terms, a straight-A cheerleader in spandex and kohl-rimmed Cleopatra eyes, the kind of thick Mexican makeup my mother called *loud* and forbade us.

I'd liked her immediately.

I was a scholarship kid from a family of the quietly poor. "Check white," my father always anxiously insisted when we'd bring the school forms home. *Such beautiful pale skin, m'ija,* my mother would say. *Like milk, this skin. You can go places. You can marry anyone.*

Act white. Talk white—and not just white, but the upper-middle-class white we were so far from being: reserved, smooth-voiced, refined. "Would you please pass the pasta?" I had to say at dinner, and my mother would say, "Of course, dear," and hand me the blackened pot of macaroni and cheese. No Spanish spoken in the house. No playing in the sun—do you want to look like a farmworker? I hung back, watched people.

So I'd grown up quiet, a good listener, which made me an attentive audience for Liz's monologues, all starring her: Liz telling off a rich white girl at the prom; Liz trumping a Harvard-bound boy in pre-calculus; Liz back-talking her supervisor at the Gap, who'd suggested that she tone down her makeup. If he could find someone else who brought in the revenues she did, then please, by all means. She fascinated me, taught as I was to keep my head down, work hard, follow rules, bite my tongue. My good grades and politeness seemed of a piece to me, so used to staying in the shade. Liz, whose bold smoky voice cracked out exactly what she thought, had been accepted at UT with a full scholarship. She would major in French and drama. She slept with anyone she wanted and never felt guilt. She wanted to be an interpreter for the UN.

Instead she had a baby, and then was killed three years later in a bar shooting. I'd been in grad school at UTSA by then. I hadn't gone to the funeral; what would have been the point? I knew no one from her life. We'd only been close for a year.

But that year. On Halloween she'd dressed me up. She crumpled fists full of my hair with her foam-covered hands to make it wild like hers. Her kohl rimmed my eyes and cast its long curling line out toward my temples, and she painted my mouth with deep lipstick the color of blood. Like a placid doll, I let her do it all, secretly thrilled, throbbing with the beauty and power I could see reflected in her full-length mirror and her boyfriend's eyes: her black miniskirt, fishnet stockings, my heels, his black leather motorcycle jacket unzipped to my rib cage with nothing beneath. I'd always been tall, gawky, shy. "Willowy," she said, blending blush across my cheek with her fingers.

Sixth Street was a carnival, a Mardi Gras, eight blocks of human crush, and we pushed our bodies through the crowds from club to club. Men stopped, turned, murmured obscenities and flattery as I kept walking. "I knew it," Liz beamed, ordering all the drinks. Behind me, threading our way through a loud dark bar, she burst out laughing. "You even *walk* different," she said. "You're walking like a model. It's infecting you, chica." We sat and drank. I could hardly speak, hypnotized, intoxicated with this power you could just decide to wear. She hooted. "You're bad. You're so bad. You just don't know it yet." We drank, and danced, the smoke folding itself into our hair and clothes. In the bathroom we watched a man and woman fuck against the wall. Liz flicked her cigarette butt at the man's ass. "Treat her right, pendejo," she said.

But that was the only time I let Liz dress me up. I retreated back into forgettable unrevealing clothes, my scrubbed Ivory-girl face, my low smooth ponytail, my don't-watch-me walk. Sometimes Liz laughed about it. "You can lead a horse to water," she'd say, her dark eyes glinting. Sometimes she'd be angry, taunting. "You're too damn polite," she'd spit. "Too soft. Too nicey-nice. Life's gonna getcha." But she was the one life got.

Too damn soft. Too nice. I finished the last dish and wiped my hands on the yellow towel. I went into the bathroom and pulled my brown eye-pencil from its flowered pouch. My face looked back at me: clean, pretty, aging. Scared. Large dark eyes, a wide pink mouth, mild laugh lines, crow's feet, quick-silvering brown hair pulled back. A kind face, a mom's face on a commercial, the face of a thoughtful, generous, good-humored woman, the kind of woman who reads Elizabeth Berg novels and cries during *Masterpiece Theater*, who'd abandoned grad school for love and children and a big, cool yard that stretched down to the lake.

Slowly, carefully, I drew on lips dark as a bruise. I penciled on hard, fatal eyes. I pulled the elastic band from my hair and shook it loose. *Chinga te*, I thought. *Chinga te*. I tried to remember everything about Liz: how she moved, her tone of voice. I wanted to be, for a quarter of an hour, a vessel for her spirit, to channel her like she believed we channeled the dead, her curandera trips a place I was too afraid to follow. When I walked back to the kitchen, I led with my hips, my face a face of stone.

I pulled the phone book from its place in the neat row with the cookbooks and books on nutritional healing. I flipped through the white pages until a surname stopped me, and I ran my fingernail down the dark column. When I dialed, a young woman's voice answered hello.

"May I speak with Michelle Ingram, please?" I said. Polite, even now.

"This is Michelle."

"Oh." I sat down suddenly in the cane chair, my left palm flat on the table's cool white tile. "This is Rosa Herrera." No response. "Victor's wife?" There was a long pause. Birds were singing.

"Okay," she finally said. "Why are you calling?"

"I thought maybe you could tell me what you were thinking." I waited, tracing the grooves between tiles with my index finger. Up, left, down, right. A square. Then the next square. Another square. Another. "Why you'd ask a married man to leave his wife for you."

"Look," she said carefully. Gauging how angry, how crazy I might be. "I'm very sorry—"

"I'm sure you are," I said. "But your sorries aren't interesting to me. What's interesting to me is why you did it." She was silent. What did she think of me? What would I have thought, at her age? "Michelle, you've met me. We've talked at parties. You've seen our children." And I'd seen her, a pretty white girl, tan and smiling, with hair like honey and tight low-cut t-shirts in bright orange, bright pink.

"Yes. Yes, I'm sorry," she said.

My hand was moving faster and faster, tracing out the squared edges of tiles all over the table. I closed it into a fist. Liz. I thought of all the bracelets the kids were wearing now, the ones that made Victor and me laugh: WWJD? They stood around talking about how trashed they'd gotten over the weekend, fuck this, fuck that, their silver WWJD bracelets flashing in the sun. I closed my eyes. What would Liz do? I cleared my throat.

"Then what was it you were thinking, exactly?" I said. "Did you think that we weren't real? That we were just one-dimensional, the boring wife and kids?" This was, in fact, exactly what I feared we had become: kept promises, obligations. The way Victor and I sat at this table every Saturday afternoon with our datebooks and pens in our hands, hashing out a mutually acceptable week. "Did you think we were just obstacles, just cardboard cutouts in your way?" I gripped the edge of the table like only my outline held me together, like a breath or a fingernail's flick could topple me.

"No, of course not," she protested. She sounded surprised, almost hurt. "No, I—"

"How *did* you think of us, then? I'm so curious. What could have been going through your mind?"

I could hear her breath drawing slowly in.

"To tell the truth, I didn't think of you at all. I mean, I knew Victor was married, but I just didn't think about it." I hated that she called him Victor. What happened to Dr. Herrera, Professor Herrera? Did he tell them to call him Victor? "I didn't mean to hurt anybody. I just didn't think about it."

"It?" I snapped. "We're not an it. We're not a state of being: *married, with children*. I'm a person, and our two children are people, and all three of us love Victor." My voice caught on his name.

Out the window, on the top of the ivy-draped fence, a bright green lizard fanned out its red throat like a moon, like a hot living jewel.

"It's not like it was personal," she said. "I never imagined—"

"Yes, I see that," I said. "I see that you never imagined. But that's what I'm going to help you do now. I know Victor has already told you no, turned you down. He came straight home and told me." She started to say something, but I kept on. "I want you to imagine your collateral damage. Clearly. I want you to know that you've hurt me, a real person. That to meet me and smile at me and then proposition my husband is like slapping my face. It's like saying, 'You couldn't possibly be anything worth staying for—'"

"It wasn't like that—"

"It was exactly like that."

"No, no, it wasn't. I swear. He just seemed so nice, and sometimes he seemed sort of sad, or lonely," she said. "Like maybe he wasn't completely happy, you know, in the marriage. It's nothing about you."

"Bullshit," I said. "It's exactly about me, and my complete irrelevance in your eyes." My hand pressed down on the table. "And of course Victor's nice, for God's sake. He's very nice. To everyone. To old ladies, and dogs, and silly doctoral students who come up after class with ridiculous questions they've made up precisely so they'll have a reason to talk to him." I heard her quick intake of breath. "And of course he's sad sometimes, or lonely. We all are, sometimes. One day you'll grow up and know that." A blue jay landed, its beak thrusting into the ivy, but the lizard had disappeared. "I can imagine you," I continued softly. "Don't think I can't imagine you. I can see everything about you. Your comfy apartment, your seriousness, your nice car your parents pay for, the way each time he made eye contact and smiled after you made some comment you'd feel a little jump."

"Hey, hang on—"

"The way you started to think about the building, all deserted at night, and how convenient his office would be, with its lock and its desk and its armless swivel chair, how you dedicated your pathetic little orgasms to him, alone at night, sending them up like prayers." This time her gasp was shocked and angry. "The double entendres you put in your e-mails, which you wrote and erased and rewrote. Don't think there's a thing about you I can't imagine, " I said. "But this phone call is so your selfish little brain can begin to imagine me." I paused. What was there to say? "To imagine a good woman, Michelle. A grownup, a woman in love, who's been in love for eleven years now. Someone with a lot more than you can see at first glance—" No, too defensive. "Someone so compelling that her husband came straight home after that reception and told her all about you and your ridiculous invitation." Yes. Better. "Because he's never, never been interested in you. He doesn't even find you attractive, with your bland obvious good looks, like some character on TV. He's bored by your type," I said.

It was a lie. He'd hung his head, looked away, said that she was pretty, smart. That yes, he'd thought of making love to her.

My whole body seemed to sway against the table.

Then I saw Liz's dark eyes flashing over the rim of her coffee cup. I heard Liz's voice: *You better get ruthless someday, baby, or the big fish gonna eat you up.*

My voice came out tough and even. "Girls like you happen every semester, Michelle. Dime a dozen. It's one of the more tedious aspects of teaching, really." I made my laugh light and amused. "How does it feel to be banal?" I asked. "Oh, don't answer; I don't care. I just want you to think, the next time you're hot for a married man, that you're going to hurt a woman, a good woman, and you might ruin the lives of little children, whether you mean to or not, whether you like to tell yourself you're a nice person or not. And even if he's not like Victor, even if he's the sort who does leave his wife for you, you will never feel safe, Michelle, never secure, and you'll never, ever get over the guilt at the real people whose hearts you've broken, whose lives you've devastated. Whose—"

"I'm a Catholic," she burst out suddenly. Her voice broke, and she started to cry. "I don't know what I was thinking. I'm a Catholic. I have a boyfriend, even."

Now. Quick, sure. I closed my eyes. "You will not call my husband. Not at his office, not at home. You will not e-mail him. You will not sign up for his classes." I saw the crowds parting as I walked, felt the long smooth power of my own legs carrying me, heard Liz's low laugh pulsing me forward. "If you see my husband at a party, you will leave. There will be no contact, ever again."

"Yes, yes, okay," she gulped. She sobbed loudly. "I'm Catholic, for God's sake—"

I hung up.

Out the window, the jay was gone, and so was the lizard. Only the blanket of ivy swung lightly against the fence. I saw Liz's fathomless eyes black with pride, her laughing mouth dark like a wound. The breath seared back into my lungs, and I took great gulps of it.

The house was still. My breathing slowed.

And then I closed my eyes again. I could see just how he'd looked that first fall day when I'd lingered after class, my arms full of books, my simple clothes pressed, my buffed nails neat with clear glaze. A rich September haze hung over the room. His dark eyes glanced up warmly as he opened his hands to me, the gold band shining and shining.

Personal Effects

At first Louise thought they were all one girl, all his daughter—those girls who appeared singly with him on the crowded subway platform where Louise waited each evening. They all wore the same olive-green parka; its fur-rimmed hood obscured the color of their hair. They were roughly the same height; the top of the hood always nearly reached his chest. He always clasped their shoulders and steered them onto subway cars: slender pale girls, eleven or twelve or thirteen, all with the same pink, pillowed lips and the same dark eyes that peered out, vague and unfocused, from beneath spikes of matted fake fur.

But then small differences emerged. One evening, the girl had green eyes: Louise was sure of it. Another night, the girl's skin was the deep amber of honey. And then one looked anxious instead of sedate, her glance darting across the platform, her feet dragging when his clamped hand steered her into the mouth of the waiting subway car.

Not that a real daughter couldn't drag her feet. Louise had done so often, long ago, and her father's or her mother's mouth would tighten into a sour line the way the man's had. But the hands on her shoulders had always been clean. His were begrimed, the nails rimmed with darkness, and his flat pale eyes were rimmed with darkness, too.

In Pakistan, in a place called Swat, the Taliban was destroying girls' schools—169 of them, to be exact, or so she'd read in the morning paper. To punish a girl for dancing, they'd pocked her with bullets, dragged her down a dirt road for a quarter of a mile, and left her broken body lying there—"splayed," the *Times* had said—in the dust of the village square. As an example to other girls.

Louise didn't know why she still bought the paper each morning, why she read it on the way to work. It always depressed her, and she was only twenty-six, too young to arrive at the office already deflated by the world.

Entering the law firm where she worked, she tried to affect a jaunty *bon vivant* bounce. But she wasn't Jon Stewart, who could find a way to laugh about terrible things. She wasn't Lena Dunham, who'd turned her liberal arts education and ennui to good account. She was just a girl who felt obliged to keep up with world events, to pull her civic weight as a grownup, and so she bought the *Times* each morning from a machine on the way to the station and read, seated on the bench, until her train arrived. Around her, voices echoed off the tiles. It was warm or cold, depending on the season, but there was always the strange underground smell of fuel.

Louise was an old-fashioned, peculiar name, which suited her. There had never been other Louises in her classes at school, as there were always Emilys and Courtneys and Brittanys. No one named a daughter Louise anymore. Her mother had chosen it as a tribute to the sculptor Louise Nevelson. Yet when Louise explained this to people, no one knew who that sculptor was.

Louise's mother was herself a noted painter, a conceptual feminist who had once strewn and glued her clipped black pubic curls onto a portrait of Nixon (oil on Masonite, 20" x 24") and whose reputation had listed along on the waning notoriety ever since. Louise's father, an anthropologist whose fieldwork was in Guatemala, had rarely been home. When he was, her parents fought and drank and would disappear into their bedroom for entire weekends, coming out only to make platters of hors d'oeuvres, smile mysteriously at Louise, and disappear again. She would wander among her mother's easels and half-finished canvases in the clear light that fell from the high, mullioned windows.

Amid the turpentine and tumult, Louise discovered a passion of her own: order. Even as a small child, she had liked to arrange things by category, lining up her parents' cluttered objects— clay shards, bones, stained paintbrushes—in rows according to size or color. Symmetry had felt like a revelation to her, a kind of measured justice, a way of paying sufficient attention to each particular thing. Standing before the open silverware drawer, immune to time, she would use her fingers like tweezers, neatening the jumble into tidy stacks: tines upon tines, the bellies of spoons nestled into fellow spoons.

As she grew older, she would sift through the drifts of mail her mother tossed on the counter, sorting it for recycling or the shredder or her parents' bill pile. Soon she began to write and sign the checks herself. She tidied the rooms of the drafty loft apartment. After consulting a manual, she would often perform small repairs with tools that otherwise languished in a red plastic toolbox under the sink.

"My little hausfrau," her mother would say, smoothing her hand over Louise's dark hair, pinching her soft cheek, paying complete attention to her for a few moments. "My little CPA."

When Louise became a secretary after graduating from an expensive private college, her parents were dismayed. They'd had expectations. They'd imagined she'd go on to the Kennedy School of Government or at least work in a gallery or publishing. They hadn't raised her in Soho for this.

"You mean administrative assistant?" her mother's well-meaning friends would sometimes ask at openings and parties, nodding encouragement.

"No," Louise would say, smiling. "Just a secretary."

She liked the modest, old-fashioned sound of the word *secretary* and sometimes even wished that *office girl* were still in vogue. She liked office girls, liked to watch them move crisply about their immaculate offices in smart dark pumps and smooth skirts on the Turner Classic Movies channel, which she watched at home alone in the evenings, eating microwaved pad thai. She loved typing, filing, organizing other people's messy desks and days into orderly grids, everything balanced, everything clear. She found comfort in the constant tide of tasks to be performed each day. She especially liked that expression about Ginger Rogers dancing just as well as Fred Astaire, but backwards and in high heels. It was just a fact. Women had to work harder, then and now, and her mother's paintings, the vulvic porcelain of Judy Chicago, and the squashy, disgusting soft sculptures of Eva Hesse hadn't done much to change that.

Not that Louise wasn't grateful. The benefits of Title IX had accrued to her in high school, where she'd been revered on the soccer team for her fierce, precise hip-checks. With one quick thrust of her pelvis, Louise could knock an opponent off stride. She was skilled at choosing her moment, administering the blows at just the right times, magical, invisible, unseen by referees. She'd been filled with optimism then, writing research papers like "The Role of Women in Society Today" and "A Woman President: Possible Here?"

In college, during the summers, she and her friends had interned at NOW and Planned Parenthood. "Direct action!" they had yelled on the streets of New York, pumping their fists in opposition to the wars in Iraq and Afghanistan, which had gone ahead and happened anyway.

In the midst of the recession, she'd graduated with an unhelpful double major in art history and anthropology. She'd been unemployable. No one had wanted her version of what thousands of other bright young women offered. Her organizational skills finally got her the job at the law firm.

"Superb," her supervisors said, paying complete attention to her for a moment as they signed her evaluation forms. She was known for her meticulous copyediting. "Invaluable."

Disillusioned, she thought, sitting on the hard metal bench at the subway stop in the evenings, gazing around at the fellow passengers awaiting their trains. *Invisible.*

She stared absently at the man. Where did he take them, evening after evening? Why had the girl with the black knapsack been crying, and why did no one else on the platform seem to notice? Louise had read in a recent exposé that one out of three runaway girls was approached by a sex trafficker within forty-eight hours of leaving home. She imagined herself down at the precinct station, explaining her suspicions to a police officer, whose handwriting would begin to slow as he eyed her skeptically, as if she were just another paranoid young woman who lived alone and watched too much *Law & Order*.

Video cameras swiveled their black eyes everywhere, but no one was really watching. All over New York, cameras swung from side to side, but no one checked the tapes until afterward, when it was too late.

And then there was the tiring fallout from the efficient little affairs conducted by the unmarried junior partners at her firm, who were very happy to buy Louise flowers privately and meet her in hotels privately and do very private things to her—until informing her, quite discreetly, as they picked up the check for one final extravagant dinner at an out-of-the-way place, that the women they were officially seeing were surgeons and socialites and tenure-track marine biologists, not secretaries. But thank you very much for the wonderful times, and they hoped she understood.

Louise did understand. She understood it all. She studied *Mad Men* to learn how smoothly a smile could fit over the face. She slid one over her own, pressing her cheeks upward with her fingertips in the mirror until the whole production looked unflappable, serene. Oil on masonite. She went back to work without a murmur, without so much as a stern squint.

But there was a certain exhaustion that came with it all.

It was inevitable that the man should eventually notice Louise. He was there on the platform once or twice a week, either with one of the young girls or alone, and she sat on the bench every weeknight, clockwork, casting her glance around.

One night, he was by himself, hands shoved deep in the pockets of his jacket. His pale eyes met hers through the jostling crowd, and she was too stunned or tired to look away. He was not bad-looking, she saw. Handsome, actually, and about her age. But his features were too lean, carved, jutting, as if he used drugs or just needed someone to cook for him. There was something feral and alarming about his eyes. But they also held something hypnotic. A song. A charm. A promise.

Some of the attorneys at the firm had the same gaze. Louise had learned to look away. But the man on the subway platform kept staring at her, a small smile curled at the edge of his lips, and she felt herself falling into the dark pinpoints of his pupils.

Her train came first, and she moved onto it with quick relief, her heart pounding, breath rushing between her lips, knowing he was still watching her from behind. Her ankles and calves in their stockings felt bare and revealed, caressed by a chill hand.

Women were being raped in the Congo, Louise read. Far away, across an ocean, in a hot place, men raped women and put knives in their vaginas. Sometimes they used machetes to cut fetuses out of the women's wombs.

She didn't understand how everyone else could manage to read the news each morning, their faces so bland and calm. She'd arrive at the plush law offices trembling, nauseated. But hers was just the ineffectual outrage of a small, unimportant piece in a vast, unblinking machine. There were no protests here, no marches. She knew that now. The great, moneyed world spun on. So she smoothed her hair and fetched coffee and typed briefs.

One day a senior partner leaned comfortably on the thick mahogany counter and said, as if inviting a confidence, "Do you know why I bought my wife a Mercedes for her birthday?"

Louise smiled like Joan on *Mad Men*. "No. Why?" she said, as if she were genuinely intrigued.

"Because I *can*," he said, and sauntered off, and it felt like the hot stinging spatter of grease on her arm when she made eggs alone in her apartment for dinner.

One evening the man on the subway platform yelled. His loud voice rasped, and his pale eyes glinted with fury and pleasure. "No, you can damn well learn to hold onto your things." His hands gripped the girl's shoulders. "I'm not dragging you around the city looking for some fucking bag."

The child sniffled, and the skin above her lip was mottled pink. She pleaded with him in a voice too soft to hear. But the man's voice was plainly audible, as if he didn't care who witnessed the altercation, as if he *wanted* to be heard, to be watched and admired as he bullied a child half his size. He shook her. "Maybe you'll hang onto your shit from now on."

People drew quietly away with small motions of their feet. There was a strange, ragged violence about the man, something helter-skelter in the blaze of his washed-out eyes. Louise wondered if he carried a knife. A gun.

She wondered what had been inside the girl's lost bag. Makeup, jewelry, a diary, a phone? Pictures of her family, three pairs of clean underwear, a locket her sister had given her? But perhaps the bag's specific contents didn't really matter—perhaps it was just the very fact of its being hers that counted so much. Her personal things. Perhaps that was the loss that hurt.

Louise, too, kept her distance from the pair, vibrating with anger and something like fear: fear for the girl, fear of what would happen if someone intervened. If she herself intervened, if the man turned his pale eyes on her.

Then their train came, and the man and girl disappeared.

"Nothing, really," she said into her phone.

Her mother called once every few weeks. Louise muted the television and stared at its silent screen: the men in their suits, the girls in dresses with small waists and flaring hems, their supple necks held with a vulnerable poise Louise rarely saw in the necks of real-life women. Like prey, but with a certain dignity.

Her mother talked about the holidays, enumerating which dinners Louise should plan to attend, which relatives were coming in from out of town, which eligible young men might be there. Louise jotted the dates down on the little notepad that always sat on the coffee table. Later, she would enter them into her calendar. She would arrive on time with a casserole and leave before anyone got truly drunk. She would take a taxi back home through the frigid darkness and let herself into her quiet apartment with relief.

One evening the girl's forehead was bruised. One evening the girl's eyes looked hollow and old.

On the day before Thanksgiving, the manager of the secretarial staff, a pretty woman in her fifties with a sharply cut blond bob and tailored suits, sat down with Louise in the office and informed her quietly and kindly that the firm regretted having to let a few of the newer girls go. It was the economy. The manager had waited until the end of the workday to tell her.

Because I can, Louise remembered the partner saying. She packed up her things—framed photographs, a hairbrush, a snow-globe of Venice—into a box.

Out on the street, Louise looked down into her box of personal effects. So much detritus. Another self that was over now. She dropped it into a trashcan's wide round mouth.

Her feet took her automatically down the sidewalk toward the subway station. *Get ahold of yourself*, is what those practical girls on TCM would say. Losing the job was a blow, yes, but tomorrow she could update her resumé. On Black Friday she could buy a new suit. Perhaps she would have it tailored. She had six months' of living expenses saved in her bank account, just as Suze Orman advised. She would be fine. She would be fine. Wind whipped bitterly into her eyes, which leaked.

Underground on the subway platform, it was warmer, but the smells of fuel and food and soured sweat felt too intimate inside her nostrils. She wished she had a handkerchief to press over her face. Lilac water. Rose water. Gardenias. When a short, heavy woman shoved past her, Louise swayed in her pumps. The crowd swelled. The night before a holiday was always busy. Louise pushed her way to the very edge of the platform.

She closed her eyes. Humans stank. Subway trains stank. It all stank. But the train would be here soon and it wouldn't matter. She tried to remember what she had in the cupboard, in the refrigerator.

When she opened her eyes, he was there, only a few yards away. He had no young girl with him. He had spotted Louise and was threading his way through the other bodies toward her. His pale blue eyes were riveted on hers. They sparked like a welding torch.

She closed her eyes again.

And then she could feel him beside her, very close, his scent the hot flare of chemicals: jet fuel, old tires burning, methamphetamine cooked in a crumbling house—and suddenly she felt the warm lump of him mashed against her hip, through the tweed of the skirt she'd pressed just that morning. She kept her eyes closed and stood motionless. She felt his breath on the side of her face and on the side of her neck where her scarf gapped. The air from his mouth smelled like chewing gum, cold and sharp, a shiv of mint. The train drew closer in the tunnel, rumbling.

With her eyes shut, she didn't know if it was his train or hers. She imagined his hand clamped on her shoulder, guiding her into the waiting doors like jaws about to close. She saw, inside the dark veils of her lids, all the faces of the girl-children who'd stepped onto trains with him, and she imagined herself gathering them all together, safe, nestled together under blankets, and crawling in with them, spoon against spoon, and closing the drawer, closing it forever.

And then she saw herself cooking eggs alone in her apartment at night, saw herself in the dark bed alone, rubbing her fingers between her legs. He was too thin, too thin. He pulsed against her, up and down, firmly, his movements hidden by the crush of bodies around them. The video cameras couldn't see. Louise was just one girl like a thousand other girls, interchangeable.

She opened her eyes. The train was drawing very close, its mechanical thunder drowning out all human sounds, its small light just visible in the tunnel's black mouth. The man was saying something soft like a sigh, the warm air inside him moving out against her skin. He ground himself onto the firm bone of her hip, and the breath from his lips pushed against her cheek and throat in small staccato bursts as he moved faster and faster, urgent—until, with a sudden sharp gathering, her hips remembered all they once had learned, and pushed back.

All the Time in the World

"But how much hair can there really be," my mother asked, "around a lady's poo-hole?"

"I couldn't say," I lied.

We were on the phone, discussing my older sister's newest career *du jour*. Annie was in cosmetology school. She had reached the unit on waxing.

Our mother, Priscilla, had been raised Mennonite in rural Indiana, and she still retained a sort of otherworldly, wide-eyed disbelief about the human race and its ways. She'd relaxed religiously during her three years of rebellion with our father—a bona fide hippie from San Francisco who'd gotten off the Greyhound in Indianapolis and been served fried eggs by a pretty young thing—and then (after that particular disaster ended) she'd enjoyed twenty-two more years of stable wedlock to our stepfather, a kindly banker who hadn't minded a house full of girls, as he called us. Now a comfortably mild-mannered Presbyterian, and for the last two years a widow, she lunched with ladies, played tennis, and took a yearly cruise, but it was all a sort of plump, staid, midwestern version of the country-club dream. She read magazines about gardening, not fashion.

The concept of the Brazilian wax shocked Priscilla, and candor—an artless generosity with the unasked-for detail—was both my sister Annie's gift and her fault.

Mine was discretion, and after a tentative foray into coming out as bisexual, which my mother could barely comprehend, I'd retreated. Priscilla's horrified eyes showed me exactly how far acceptance reached. I left it alone.

During our mandatory twice-weekly phone chats, we talked instead about her flowerbeds and the latest movie we'd both seen, which was always a chore to determine, since she preferred light romantic comedies, and I liked aimless French films where everyone ends up realistically miserable. *Cute* was Priscilla's watchword, and she peppered her calm life with experiences ranging all the way from *pleasant* to *nice*. When American advertisers tapped into the repressions of fifty million middle-aged women by using the words *decadent* and *indulge*, our floral-upholstered mother did not wad her ears with cotton and rope herself to the mast: she plunged headfirst into a molten chocolate pudding cake.

My job as a public defender scared her. It scared me, too, and when we talked, I left out most of the details. Atlanta was not Carmel, Indiana, the upscale suburb of Indy where my sister and I had grown up, all pretty malls and golf courses and places to get your nails done. Atlanta had those things, too, as well as museums and history and art and live music I rarely had time to go hear, but in Atlanta, terrible things happened, and my job was to fight for the people who might or might not have done them.

Priscilla trusted my toughness, my straight-through-law-school drive. She trusted my sharp charcoal suits and the way I slapped my briefcase down on the dining table when I visited at holidays. She trusted the steely way I refused every little whipped-cream treat she offered, drinking only iced tea and then, after six p.m., iced vodka. She trusted that my 401K was as pregnant as I was not. About me, she had no worries. At least, not the professional kind.

My sister, though, had inherited our real father's sweet hippie charm and wandering ways. Where my hair was a dark, razored bob, Annie had long surfer-girl curls that swung down to the small of her back. Her generous pink lips were always glazed with plumper, and she wore Indian peasant blouses cut low to show the inner curves of her breasts. She had tattoos, wore a toe ring, and ambled easily in her sandals. Gentle and feckless, she was what I had smashed in myself. I'd grown up watching Priscilla agonize over her. Annie was a trouble to our mother and a thorn in her side. I'd decided long ago to be the good girl. No worry, no expense. Annie was all trouble, inviting and delectable. She was the kind of girl I picked up in bars. My mouth was a matte red line that smeared off on their skin.

My sister had already learned nails, facials, and hair, and now her class at the cosmetology school was coming down the home stretch. She would be licensed soon, and that's why—according to my own private analysis of the case—she was calling our mother with vivid details of genital waxing: to shock and horrify Priscilla, who would then talk her out of continuing. Because if Annie did continue, it would mean she'd finally finish something, and then she'd have no excuses. The world would expect her to punch a clock, get in line, be a grownup. At thirty-one, she'd avoided all that so far. She had sweet, lazy friends who'd managed to drift prettily around until they fell in love with some guy in a band or an investment firm who would marry and support them, and she saw no reason it couldn't happen to her. After all, she gave a great massage. She could blow glass and grow organic vegetables and still turn six cartwheels in a row. She was winsome and fetching and all those pretty words, and she'd always be good arm-candy at parties and eventually a whimsical mom.

In Atlanta, Vietnamese girls with translucent skin and tiny Tupperware lunches stacked in the salon's mini-fridge did my nails once a week for twenty bucks, and sometimes we'd fuck in the break-room after the shop closed.

"Getting beautiful is the most important thing in the world," Annie had breathed to me over salads at the Cheesecake Factory when we were both at home for Christmas. "After spirituality, I mean. And taking care of the environment." She widened her eyes. "And if I can help people do that, my life will have meaning." My very presence put her on the defensive. "And I'll always be employed, so I won't be a burden on society."

"You're a real Gandhi," I said. "You're Nelson fucking Mandela." Priscilla had gone off to the restroom, fussing and clucking over our lack of appetite.

"And you're always such an asshole, Rose. Why is that?"

Now her words came back to me as my mother fretted into my ear. We each vexed our mother in our own way. We grieved her. Why couldn't we be as we were? When we were little girls, we played happily together for hours within the drooping embrace of the mulberry tree, enclosed in its leafed and twisted branches and the vivid, fey little worlds Annie would make up. Priscilla would come out to the backyard with freshly baked lemon cookies. As a family, it was our finest hour. Priscilla never recovered from its passing.

"I just don't know what to do with that child," she said.

"Well, Mom, if she wants to paint hot wax around ladies' poo-holes, let her."

"Oh, don't say that. I can't imagine. Just think, having someone do that in public." The shock was still fresh in her voice. "They do sterilize everything, don't they?"

"I think so."

"I hope she doesn't catch anything." She sighed. "Our poor Annie."

"She's fine. She's getting an education." I thought of law school at IU and the assholes I'd had to steer around.

"Maybe she should come home."

"Mom."

"She says she misses everything. She says there's a lot of crime in Savannah." God, my sister knew how to push Priscilla's buttons—Priscilla, who'd love nothing better than to install both of us back in our childhood bedrooms and bake muffins each morning. Birds would presumably chirp; sunlight would glint on our hair. The potted herbs would nod gaily from the windowsill, and when we laughed, our teeth would flash white twinkles. We'd be *enrobed* in her motherly care.

"Mom, there's crime everywhere. Savannah's a nice town. It's no more dangerous than Indy. Less, probably."

"She misses her friends, she says."

"Annie's fine. She can talk to her friends on the phone."

"If I bought her a plane ticket, she could be home tomorrow."

"Yeah. She could." I tried to recall all the places Annie had flown back from over the years: Santa Fe, Portland, LA, Miami, Seattle—a dozen different attempts at finding her métier once Ball State spat her out. I wondered how chaotic my own life would look if I'd ever let slip on the phone my fear or disillusionment, if our mother had ever bought my way home. I remembered biting my own hand once, in my second month here, to keep myself from calling her.

"I could get online right now and order her a ticket. If I got United, I could get miles."

"You could. You could do that." I was too tired to argue. I'd argued all day, and this was hardly life or death. I sipped my drink quietly, so Priscilla couldn't hear the ice cubes rattle.

My apartment was cool and dark. Outside it was still hot and bright, in the nineties.

"She could stay here at the house," she continued, "until she figures out what's next. There's no reason to rush, you know."

"That's an idea," I said.

"Yes, I know it's an *idea*," she said, her voice suddenly spiked with irritation, "but what do you think?" She'd caught a whiff of being fobbed off, of being handled. "I mean *actually*. What do you actually think?"

I sighed. "You want my opinion?"

"Yes, I do."

"Well, honestly, Mom, I think you should stay out of it."

I heard her exasperated sigh.

"Leave Annie alone. If you bail her out now, she won't finish, and then she'll be back to square one. All that time and money wasted. If you leave her alone, it might suck for a week or two, but she'll get through it, and then she'll have her license, and she can get a decent job . . ." Suddenly I flashed, the born lawyer sussing out her jury's secret desires. "At a spa or someplace."

"A spa," Priscilla murmured. There was a long pause.

"She'd have great job security. It's a forty-billion-dollar-a-year industry now. She could find a really nice place."

"That would certainly be a pleasant work environment," our mother said slowly. I could almost hear the fountain quietly splashing in her brain, feel the soft terrycloth around her shoulders. It sounded pretty good to me, too, twenty-nine and alone in a city that roughed me up on a weekly basis, leaving me torn and rancid with failure.

"And it would be safe," I pointed out.

"Safe." Our mother's voice brightened, rallied. She had just needed to be convinced. "Maybe you're right. Maybe she just needs to work through this. Every job has parts that aren't great, you know." She sighed. "Parts you didn't want or know about when you signed up for it." I wondered if she was thinking of waitressing or of being a mom.

"Exactly," I said. "No job's perfect." And there in my drink I suddenly saw swinging toward me the dark, wounded eyes of my eighteen-year-old client who'd been sentenced that afternoon, and the way I'd collapsed with my back against my office door when I'd gotten back inside alone, sliding down until my charcoal-suited ass was on the floor, and cried into my hands. I gulped the vodka down. "You just try to do what you can."

"But I wish you two girls were happier," Priscilla said, her tone high and laced with that maternal sluice of righteous disappointment and the generous, desperate, selfless warmth I'd tried to wean myself from for so long. I could hear the loneliness in her voice, too. She was struggling against her own hunger to call Annie home. Mixed doubles and ladies' teas were no substitute for a daughter you could put your arms around. "I just want to see you both settled down and happy."

I cleared my throat. My ice had all melted. I swirled my glass and drank what was there.

A Mother Who Means Well
Is Harder to Lose

The best thing you could say about my mother's cooking is that it was well intentioned. When we lived in London, she even took a gourmet cooking course and ran up huge grocery bills, ruining duck and lamb and filet mignon. My father and little brother and I would sit at the beautiful table—candlelight and fan-folded linen napkins—and try not to grimace as we picked at the sodden vegetables, while she sat sipping iced tea, flipping her crossed-over leg up and down, up and down, smiling expectantly at our careful faces.

My mother herself never ate after four o'clock in the afternoon. Eating late is the fastest way to get your weight up, she liked to tell us.

"Look," she'd say, patting her belly and turning side to side in front of the bureau mirror, "two of you little figure-wreckers, and still flat, flat, flat." Even around the house, she was glamorous. Capri pants and headscarves and lipstick, and movie-star sunglasses if she went shopping.

My favorite thing was watching her get dressed for a party. She'd start two hours before liftoff with a bubble bath—"You need to feel like a queen at one of these things, sweetheart," she'd say. "They'll rip your heart out, otherwise." She would sit at the vanity in a satin slip, powder-puffing and paintbrushing until she was prettier than a city at night, shimmering and shining under the row of little white bulbs. Then she'd step into a jewel-bright ball-gown and put on her size six heels and twirl around, laughing and clapping her fine hands in a little rush of excitement. My father would shoe-horn himself into his black patent leather shoes and fasten his cufflinks and kiss her hair, and they'd be gone in a cloud of White Shoulders.

While they were gone, the babysitter would play groceries with us, pulling things out of the refrigerator and lining them up on the counter while my brother and I took turns pushing my doll pram up and down the kitchen as if it were a cart. All too often, though, she would quickly shut a container with a pained look and set it carefully back on the shelf. My mother loved the idea of using leftovers, the concept, but somehow never quite got around to implementing it.

She had no compunction about keeping me home from school when she wanted company. She would stroke my hair in the morning until I woke up, and smile her secret smile. "Do you want a holiday?" she would whisper, and I'd laugh and jump up, wondering. Sometimes we'd stay home and bake cookies: hand cookies, my mother called them, her personal invention. After the dough was rolled out thin, she would knife carefully around the outline of my hands and then hers. Then I got to paint them with food coloring and decorate them with all the little colored sugars and glitters. I would paint wedding rings on every finger, each in a different color. "Oh yes," she'd cry out, "so lovely!" Then the baking: the house would steam up with the voluptuous smell of them, soft and sugary and buttery and browning just for us in the oven. She would eat my hands and I would eat hers, one finger at a time.

On some of my secret holidays, we'd dress up in our match-ing dresses—"More like sisters, really," she'd say—and we'd take the train downtown, wandering through bookstores and flower stalls and pastry shops, and her saying yes to everything I wanted.

Sometimes she'd have our things gift-wrapped there at the stores, and we'd carry them home on the train all tinseled and bowed as if it were Christmastime, and sit on the living room floor and open them all, exclaiming. She would gather all the wrapping paper into a bag and take it out to the trash before my father and brother came home. "He wouldn't understand," she'd say, meaning my father. My brother was too little to count.

My father was the gentlest man in the world, I thought, and handsome too, but he really didn't seem to understand. Not really. When he'd put his arm around her or try to kiss her anywhere but the hair or cheek, she'd push him away and laugh nervously. Her eyes would brighten as if in fear, and she'd glance at my brother and me and smile stiff little pleading smiles. Couldn't he see? He was hurting her, couldn't he see? It was like a ripping. Don't do that, I wanted to cry. That was later on, in Miami, before we had to move.

When the strange times happened, I learned to remember those fear-faces she made. Sometimes when we were alone in the house, I would be talking to her and she would start moving faster and faster around the kitchen, putting things down harder and harder in their drawers and cupboards, until finally she'd turn in a flash and slap me over and over in the face and shake me hard until I cried. Then she'd hold me and start to cry herself, "I'm sorry, I'm so sorry. Please don't make Mommy do that. Don't make Mommy have to do that." She would hold me until we both stopped crying. I wished for an older sister to explain it to me, explain it away, the way that later I would hold my brother in my lap and tell him that she didn't mean it. She loves you. She does.

But by that time she wasn't laughing nervously when my father put his arm around her. She was hardening all over—you could see it from across the room—and staring at him and lifting a slow eyebrow, and he was backing away grimly. She still kept a beautiful house, with beautiful rugs and furniture, but instead of just one junk drawer in the kitchen there was now a junk drawer in every room, and beware the traitor child who opened a closet or cabinet when company came. It wasn't until I grew up that I learned that some people organized things no one could see, that some houses were in order all the way down.

Even then, she made American-style Thanksgiving dinner all from scratch, with roast turkey and long egg noodles that took all morning and real mashed potatoes with the skins mixed in. Everything needed spoonfuls of salt to taste good.

But she stopped cooking altogether when my father was away. She'd order pizza, or make three batches of popcorn and buy sodas for us all, and we'd sit and watch television, the three of us huddled together on the sofa in the big family room.

He started having to travel an awful lot, my father, so that we didn't see him much except on weekends, and eventually he had to take weekend trips as well. My mother took to shopping a lot and started us at a church that met three times a week. Sometimes she even went out on her own in the evenings with some women from the church. She thought the independence would do us good. "I'm going to teach you how to cook for yourself, honey," she said, taking the TV dinners out of the freezer and turning them over to frown at the instructions. And we had sports and after-school activities by that time. So it wasn't as if our routine was interrupted much when my father finally told us that he had to get an apartment of his own. It wasn't as if very much had changed at all, my mother said. Not much at all, she would say brightly.

Looking back on it, I guess that when my father left her, she was just looking for someone to destroy her the rest of the way. I stayed for two years after she remarried, and then I ran away.

But I remember one day, peeling apples in the yard outside, making the pie that the new husband required every night, she told me the story of her first date with my father. He had picked her up in his new red convertible, with his hair all combed back and beautiful and his tie straight and his collar pressed. He picked up the twenty-year-old stewardess with her long legs and her trim ankles and her short hair fluffed up in blue-black curls, and he took her in his shiny red car to a riverbank. She had expected the dinner and movie and the usual brusque and silent attempt. But my father opened the trunk and handed her wine and two glasses, and he pulled out a watermelon, icy and huge. They walked together in their first-date clothes down toward the water, and she spread her skirt carefully on the grass. It was a yellow dress, full-skirted, and she looked like a daffodil, he told her. And after a small struggle with the opener, he uncorked the bottle, and they sat on the bank drinking their wine and carving slice after slice of the watermelon as the stars began coming out.

I think of her sometimes as I saw her last, sitting outside the little house without any makeup, her hair straggling around her neck, with a bruise on her cheekbone and a gash above her eye. I think of the wistful way she looked out at the road when she told me her story.

But the older I get, the more I think of the pretty raven-haired girl arranged on the riverbank in a spreading daffodil dress, gazing at the handsome profile that didn't expect her to cook or clean, gazing and waiting for it to turn and see her, waiting for it to love her, while the chewed-out rinds bobbed and drifted and eventually sank.

Dinner

Sacramento didn't meet her father until she was seventeen. He was not what she'd been led to expect.

For years, her mother Jojo had talk-storied him into legend—according to which he was practically a shaman, a guru: luminous, gentle, in tune with the rhythm of tides. Jojo had met him at a bar in Miami and gone backcountry camping at a beach site in the Everglades, the tent doused in mosquito repellent, the swamp full of night sounds. In the black sky: thousands of stars, like salt on velvet. What Jojo remembered were his gentle hands, his easy smile, his shining dark hair, and the way he knew the names of birds.

Those were the details she'd told Sacramento. She'd left out the fact that he was white.

Blue eyes, of all things. Flesh so pale you could see thin greenish vessels twisting through it. On the crest of his head, a flat gray plate of hair was losing ground fast. Little flesh-hammocks the color of carbon hung beneath his eyes. He smelled like illness.

That first night of their acquaintance—after dinner in the Mexican restaurant, where he'd pulled an industrial-sized plastic bottle of Tums (tropical flavors) out of his jacket pocket and set it on the table like just another condiment, where he'd asked those awkward questions about school and sports, and Sacramento, in turn, had asked him why he'd left her mama, in response to which he'd gazed very intently at a faded piñata of a parrot, its once-bright reds and greens now faded to pastels—that night, Sacramento would return to her motel room alone and stand in front of the bathroom mirror. She would stare, still shaking, at her naked gold self.

But her brown eyes, her black hair, her full lips (his were thin, the upper one just a furrowed shelf where flesh stopped), and her smooth, glowing skin were all just younger versions of her mother's. She would sigh, relieved.

This man who was her father lived two states away from the apartment she shared with her mother in St. Petersburg. She had driven in a borrowed car to meet him, ignoring the radio's reports of a tropical storm headed northwest across the Gulf. Alone and seventeen, she had driven six hundred miles, windows down, wind whipping her face and arms to numbness, the car smelling like wet salt, the radio too loud to think. She'd spent what she'd earned mopping floors at Popeye's to learn what kind of man helped make her, her cells half his.

Carefully, she had not let herself feel the hope that quivered somewhere just outside her skin, hovering: the hope that he would be pleased to know her, proud, that they could be friends—even maybe, one day, feel like family. She just wanted to see him, to recognize something of herself in the handsome dream of her mother's legend, to know that she had come from something beautiful and good. To fill the hungry hollow of not knowing.

Compulsion had drawn her across northern Florida, through Alabama, and along the line of the Mississippi Gulf Coast into a decaying beach town full of crab shacks and rusting carnival rides, where her father lived in a studio apartment eighteen blocks from the shore.

Her mother thought she was spending the long weekend at her friend Gabby's.

At her father's apartment complex, each wooden board of the staircase creaked and sank a little under her feet. The red paint on his door peeled away in long strips. She knocked, glancing around. Dark clouds were moving in over the Gulf, and the wind was a solid force against her legs.

He opened the door, blinking. He didn't seem to know who she was or why she was there. It wasn't the warm welcome she'd imagined. The odor of stale beer wafted out of his apartment.

"Mmm." He grinned. His eyes traveled up and down her body. "You look like dinner."

Her brain convulsed with fear. Maybe this was all some Internet scam, his cordial e-mail replies just a front for sex traffickers to groom and season young girls, as she'd been warned by high school bulletins and *Nancy Grace*.

But no: she was the one who'd found him, typing his name and social security number into the PeopleSearch blanks.

And if anything bad happened, her mother would save her. She was her mother's angel baby, her one pure thing: clean and wholesome and headed for success via her straight As and soccer championship and volunteer work down at the hospital on Tuesday afternoons. She would not (so went her mother's oft-narrated dream) succumb to the mistakes her mother had made.

And here stood one of her mother's old choices, the only one whose sperm had nimbly nabbed an ovum, bitten hard, and wriggled its way in.

"I'm your daughter," she said. "Remember? We talked on the phone."

At dinner, facing Sacramento across the red vinyl booth, the man who was her father asked his stiff questions, nodding in a TV imitation of paternal approval. Three Coronas later, when he finally relaxed, he began to talk about himself. He spoke as if to a buddy—truck-stop language, locker-room language—not his newfound teenaged daughter. He rambled, taking long pulls off his bottle, using words that made Sacramento glance around, embarrassed, hoping no one else could hear. He had hitchhiked eleven times across the glorious old US of A, as he put it. Picked apples in New England. Cleaned stables in Louisville. Fucked a hell of a lot of women. Now he was getting old and tired. Now he needed a warm place to land for the winter, like any other retiree.

It was a long monologue, starring himself, unspooling endlessly as if on a spool of endless paper: the countless women, the booze, the acid and pot and PCP, very good stuff, his forays into heroin and cocaine—but he preferred the mountains rising up at the horizon as the truck pulled west and actual sex, he confided, while H left you content to just sit in a dark room all day.

He was glad to be done with all that, now that meth was the thing.

"Don't get started doing that shit," he said. "That's my fatherly advice." His laugh was a croak.

At first, he couldn't remember her mother. Sacramento had to describe everything Jojo had told her about camping in the Everglades. Her voice was halting. It hurt her to say the beautiful words her mother had repeated like rosary prayers.

"Ah," he said, nodding slowly, his eyes vague. "Right. Sure." He rolled his beer between his palms. Then his blue eyes lit. "Oh, yeah. She's the one had that tattoo of a bird right down to her pussy," he said.

Sacramento choked a little on her Diet Coke.

The tattoo was a Wakinyan, a thunderbird. As a small child, Sacramento had traced its visible portions with her finger, its dark blue-black curves all wavery from pregnancy. Much later, she learned that the tattoo came from her mother's commitment-to-the-people phase—*My dad's side, Lakota, AIM, all that*, Jojo would say quickly. *Ancient history. I've moved on.* What was the point in dwelling on it? The people had never shown any commitment to her. Jojo was a severed limb no one ached for. To mark herself as someone's child, she'd let strangers pierce her until she bled. She'd had to check books out of the library to learn about her father's world.

Curled safe in the warm crook of her mother's arm, Sacramento would listen to her tales of the Wakinyan:

"And then Thunderbird grabbed Whale up in her sharp talons, plucking him from the sea. She carried him over the land, wrestling and fighting. Finally, Whale gave up his spirit. Yes, I'm sad to say it. Whale died. Wakinyan dropped him to feed the starving people down below, and they rejoiced and worshipped her."

When Sacramento was a kid, she protested. Poor Whale! After all, he was just swimming around, minding his business. To get suddenly snatched into the sky and dropped as a sacrifice wasn't fair.

Her mother would squeeze her tight and nuzzle the soft, dark child-silk of her hair. "My sweet baby," she would breathe. "My sweet, sweet baby, who thinks life's fair."

In the booth in the Mexican restaurant, the man who was Sacramento's father was squinting in reverie. "Long black hair," he said. "Big lips." He chuckled. "Knew what to do with them, too."

Sacramento pushed the mushy beans around her plate. Oozed grease pooled orange next to the rice. There was no right reply.

"Now, what was her name again?" He shifted his Corona from hand to hand. Black hairs thatched his wrists like ink cross-hatching in a nineteenth-century sketch. His gray jacket's cuffs were soiled a deeper gray.

"Her name is Jojo."

"Oh, yeah." He took a drink. "That was it."

Her mother had ended up a paralegal. Twenty-four, pregnant, an orphan, and alone, she rode Greyhounds to Paterson, New Jersey, where she lived with an aunt, waited tables, and went to night school. Sacramento couldn't remember anything about those years except the sound of Spanish like a soft and constant song, neighbors' and old ladies' voices weaving a pattern like bright lace, like a webbed hammock she could bounce in.

But her mother missed the sun. When she'd gotten her associate's degree, she packed everything they owned into a fourth-hand Corolla and drove them back down the seaboard to Florida. St. Petersburg was the only home Sacramento knew.

To the law office, Jojo wore polite clothes and SAS loafers because her feet hurt her, but on Saturdays she still went dancing in a glittery dress. On Sunday mornings, sometimes a strange man would wander out into the kitchen for coffee—but always a brown man, Cuban or Mexican or Puerto Rican, which caused Sacramento to develop certain assumptions about her mother's taste.

Some nights after her mother had gone to bed, Sacramento would slip out to the dark and silent kitchen, open the cupboard, and pour a little hill of cumin seeds into her palm. She would raise her cupped hand to her face and inhale their musky tang, licking them up and grinding them with her teeth into a bitter paste she swallowed. What compelled her to do such a weird thing, late at night, alone, she didn't know.

Sacramento had never once imagined her father would be white.

Not even to get child support had Jojo ever tried to track him down. Men knock you up and leave: that's life. Jojo knew a dozen women with the same story. The guy moves on, while you get permanently grounded with kids, bills, and a script for anti-anxiety meds.

"She was sure a sweet one," said the man who was her father.

"Yes," said Sacramento. "She is."

When she was little, her mother told her bedtime stories every night, then sang until she fell asleep. She never yelled. Now that Sacramento was seventeen and on the verge of everything, her mother would listen at the table with her chin cupped in her hand, sipping her café for as long as Sacramento wanted to talk. Before school, her mother always checked her clothes to make sure not too much skin showed. Even though she adjusted things once she was out of sight, Sacramento liked the fuss her mother made.

"Yeah, she was sweet, all right." He hacked his raspy smoker's cough and cleared his throat. His blue eyes flared. "A good tight one to pop my stick in." He laughed so loudly that a woman at the next table turned to look.

Sacramento's stomach swam, and she closed her eyes. She thought her fish tacos would spill back out onto the plate. Dishes clattered. A cart full of bus tubs rumbled by. The norteño lyrics complained about a woman's faithlessness. When Sacramento opened her eyes, her father was staring off into his memories, a smile on his thin lips.

She wondered what her mother looked like in his mind. Not a person. Just something tight.

She thought of her mother's small, tired feet, and her voice came out soft, like the sound of something crushed. "Don't talk about her."

"Huh?"

"Don't talk about my mother."

"Hey, settle down, girl." He waved his beer at her. "You're getting all strung out."

"Don't tell me what to do. And don't talk about her. You don't know anything." Her voice rose. "You don't deserve to say her name."

"You gonna preach at me?" His eyes went mean and narrow. "You gonna tell me what to do, you little cunt?"

Long ago, in Washington State, her mother had taken her to a special park built for viewing salmon. It was educational. A nature moment.

Safe on the sidelines with their paper-cup sodas and boxes of Cracker Jack, they watched the fish batter their long, meaty bodies against the rocks and man-made concrete barriers, falling back, their scales silvering off in the water.

Sacramento felt sick, fascinated by their desperation, ashamed of watching the damage they willingly did.

"Don't talk to me like that." Her voice was low. It cracked. "I'm your daughter, motherfucker. Your daughter."

"Okay, okay." He rubbed his hands together, massaged the joints a little. "You're right. Cool down, girl. I was just reminiscing."

"No, you cool down." Her voice was damp and young. She gathered up her backpack and the little lavender album of photographs she'd brought to show him: herself newborn, herself as a little girl, herself shooting to 5'9" with baby fat still on her cheeks, herself newly lean on the soccer team, then in a purple prom dress. He'd flipped listlessly through them.

She snapped the album shut and shoved it into her bag.

"Find your own ride home," she said. "I'm done." She slid toward the edge of the booth and stood up, her keys in her hand.

"No, come on. Don't go. I said I'm sorry."

"No, you didn't."

"What?"

"You never said that."

His hands opened out toward her. "I'm sorry."

She took a breath. As the seconds passed and she stood immobile, one of his hands groped toward the Tums, while the other itched across the pack of American Spirits that jutted from his jacket pocket.

"Come on," he said. "Sit down. Please."

Okay. She would be genteel, like the velvet-voiced women on the late-night movies she and her mom watched on Turner Classics. She would play the gracious hostess. Grace Kelly, Ingrid Bergman, Audrey Hepburn. She set her backpack down on the seat.

"Would you like dessert?" she asked, lowering herself to the split red vinyl. "Or coffee?"

They tried again.

It was getting late. The tables around them had emptied, and they'd run out of things to say. The norteño's polka thump was jacked up loud. They sat there not talking, waiting for the waiter to brew a pot of coffee.

Her father chewed his Tums and stared down at his scraped plate. The silence grew loud between them. Eventually he spoke. "So why'd your mother name you after the capital of California?" he asked. "Shoulda called you Tallahassee." He laughed at his own joke.

Sacramento sat very still, not caring to explain.

His face dropped. "So what'd you come here for, Tallahassee?" he said. "Really? You can see I got no money. I just got my disability every month. That's it." He cleared his throat. "If that's what you're after, I got nothing for you."

Outside, the clouds were gray and low. Thin shafts of lightning split the sky. The air felt clogged and heavy.

Sacramento sat quietly, thinking about his words and her long drive west alone.

On the stucco wall between them hung a painting of a brown Aztec warrior, his back awash in feathers. He gazed nobly off into the mountains like he owned them, and an eagle perched on his arm. At his feet, a bare-thighed woman coiled, gazing up at him adoringly, her arms around his shins. She looked sexy and pathetic. It was the same painting Sacramento had seen in Mexican restaurants in Tampa. Always before, she had wondered why people needed to see this while they ate.

Now she knew. Making men into myths and heroes was just easier.

She stared up at a piñata, a large pink egg that might once have been Humpty Dumpty. Its cardboard undergirding was enduring a state of slow collapse, the pink shreds of paper limp in the damp air. Outside, the first heavy drops were falling. She wanted a stick to bash that paper face with, to get the breaking over and done, to let the stale and putrid candy just rain down.

Her eyes sifted slowly through the strings of red chili-pepper plastic lights and the molded resin reproduction of the Mayan calendar. They landed finally on the worn-out, washed-up wreck of what her father was supposed to have been.

He reached for the brown mug of coffee and two little creamers. His hands were trembling.

He saw her seeing them shake, and he winced, the gray flesh around his eyes creasing, like he was bracing for a strike.

"I don't talk to people much," he mumbled, looking down. Trying to open a creamer, his fingers fumbled too long.

Suddenly she felt the swamping pain of his loneliness, his lifelong running, his stuffing himself with whatever available pleasure he could find. Her sympathetic tongue stung with the bitter spill of cumin. The weight of both her parents crushed her, and she couldn't breathe. She was shot through with her mother's sad dreams and courage, her boring office days, her tired small crooked feet. Her throat choked with the stench of insect repellent and the accident she was. She felt like she was underwater, drowning.

Slowly, as if of its own accord, her slim brown arm stretched across the grease-spotted paper placemats and soiled plates. She lifted the creamer from her father's shaking fingers, drew it toward herself, and peeled the foiled paper back easily with her smooth nails.

Looking down, she felt a sudden strange release, as if she were falling from a great height into the pale thick gloss of the cream.

Air rushed into her lungs. She looked up.

"I came to meet you," she said. "I don't need anything. I just came to see who you were."

She reached over and set the little container down in front of him.

The River

For 132 years in the town of Halford, North Dakota, there had secretly flowed an underground, life-giving force, a sustaining power. This force, the Ladies' Literary Society of Halford, no longer required its members to wear white gloves—though some of the most elderly ladies still did, the white kid gripped incongruously around the unapologetic aluminum poles of their walkers, their lovely pastel wool suits altered by the best tailors in Bismarck to curve snugly over their humps.

The Society no longer required the wearing of elegant hats, but it continued to meet at three o'clock on the second Tuesday of every month (a schedule instituted back in the mists of time to accommodate the social whirl of the wife, deeply coveted as a member, of an early president of Halford State), and assembly continued to rotate from one member's well-appointed home to another, where, after the little bell from Portugal had been rung by the president, after the minutes had been read and the announcements announced and the literary paper had been read aloud by its writer and discussed by all and sundry, the coffee, tea, and homemade biscuits prinked with colored icing would be served.

For 132 years, succeeding generations of ladies had upheld these customs, and this continuity had flowed like a life-giving stream under the surface of life in Halford, imprinting onto their lives the slender, tenuous joy of anticipation, the durable surety needed to surmount the dark tedium of the winters, that icy whiteness that began already by mid-December to feel utterly, inescapably permanent. With the Ladies' Literary Society of Halford, there would be something to look forward to each month, something gracious, pretty, something interesting to think about and talk about with other ladies all dressed up. It flowed beneath the visible surfaces of ordinary life, because membership was by invitation only, invitations whispered or murmured or issued in a normal voice in private tête-à-têtes, and because, as the yearly programme clearly stated under the heading "Rules," members were to make no public mention of the Society's existence. Its doings had never graced the pages of the *Halford Daily Register*. Only the best people joined.

But now it was June, and Ilse Kirchgrader had flung her windows open. Birdsong had filled the sunny little house all morning, and even with the arthritis in her knuckles, the arthritis in her hips, her ankles, even her knees now, even so, moving from room to room had been a joy—opening up the wooden folding chairs with their padded leather cushions and arranging them in rows across the carpet, wiping one final time the silver serving platters Antoinette had polished on Friday, taking the little biscuits hot from the oven, sliding them with a spatula onto the cooling rack, and then squeezing out dollops of pink and pale green from the cones. The squeezing had hurt. But still, it was a joy.

She had been so happy, when the little forest-green booklet had arrived in its unassuming envelope in January, to scan the list and find her name listed as hostess in June. During the long months without sun, the house could look dark, even dreary, but June would be perfect: wisteria would be blooming and fragrant and heavily pendent from the pergola as guests came up the walk, and she'd have made sure all the flowerboxes were stocked lushly with annuals, spicy-scented petunias and perhaps some tumbling variegated vines and other things. And she had. One front-facing window opened over the sink, and she stood with her hands in the dishwater to breathe the lifting sweet smell.

For forty-three years she had lived in the little house, just blocks down the street from the university that had offered her Tom a job fresh out of graduate school. For forty-three years she had been Mrs. Thomas Kirchgrader, wife and then widow of an esteemed professor of biology. For quite some time after they'd arrived in Halford she would clarify, upon being introduced to someone new, "I went to Wellesley." And then one day she forgot, and then never said it again.

They had planned to move from the tidy little house to something bigger when the children came. But children did not come. It was snug and just right for two, she brightly told her parents and sister many times, and really, it was much better this way. She could travel with Tom on his collecting trips, and in the evenings during the semester when he came home tired and frustrated from campus, there she would be, pretty and crisp with his scotch, ready to listen with her full attention from the opposite loveseat. She had never before imagined just how tumultuously a simple department of biology could seethe and churn and feud.

Tom had become a biologist long before the fashion changed, back when being a biologist meant being in love with nature, when it meant to be a small piece of nature wondering at all the other pieces and how they fit together. Nowadays, according to what Tom had said, it meant cells. It meant micro. It meant a lifetime in a fluorescent-lit lab, when once the lab had been only the helpful supplement to the real work, the work that went on out in the world, in the woods, in the water, where you were just a small piece walking or floating and noticing together with other pieces. When people became biologists back then, it was because they had, as children, once awakened from a sunny nap in the woods to find a deer and her fawn grazing very close upwind and lain there taking the shallowest, quietest of breaths until the two creatures had ambled delicately away. Or they'd seen a hawk swoop so close overhead they could see its separate tailfeathers tinged with red. There had been a reverence, there had been a wonder, there was wind and sun on the face. Now biology was just another indoor career for clever people, like computer science.

She had heard Tom say this in the last years, frustrated, losing ground. It was all very interesting, the tales of departmental infighting and the passionate lectures-for-one after dinner and the long collecting trips in the summers, all very interesting for years and years and then he died. And with microwaves the rest of a casserole needn't go to waste, so she kept cooking as she always had, something hot with a nice fresh salad, and cleaning as she always had (though the name of the help would change, and sometimes the girl would be from Halford and sometimes would drive in from the Fort Franklin Indian Reservation in a rickety car that embarrassed Ilse while it sat all day every Friday in front of her tidy house in its row of neat faculty houses; she often went out on Fridays). But everything was largely the same, except that there was no Tom at the center and no Mother or Father, either, of course, but her sister still called every week from Florida and they'd talk for a good hour, and there was church, too, and she had her friends, and the garden, and she read all winter long as she always had, curled in her soft flowered chair next to the unlit fire, only now a hired man came to shovel and salt the walk and driveway, Tom didn't do it. And on the second Tuesday every month there was the lovely Society meeting to look forward to.

Not that it hadn't also changed, in its way. When Ilse had first begun attending—oh, the joy of that murmured invitation from the sublimely coiffed Ellen Hewitt on the bright lawn of Christ Lutheran that Sunday afternoon!—back then, the papers had been about genuinely great books, the masterworks of literature, *Moby Dick* and *War and Peace* and Shakespeare. Ilse had once given a paper on *The Cherry Orchard*, and the questions people asked had been quite hard. But the younger women who joined and sat on the annual Text Selection Committee shook things up. They liked themes, not greatness. One year they'd read Betty Friedan and *Housekeeping* and parts of *The Second Sex*. Nowadays they read books with Spanish words mixed in and left undefined, so you didn't know quite what was happening, and practically every other main character of a novel had been abused as a child or humiliated in some crushing and formative way, which they then had to overcome by unlocking the secrets of their past. And the questions the younger members asked were sometimes tiresome, as though they'd invented the very concepts of *oppression* and *hierarchy* and *power relations* and *subversion* and had to keep saying the words many, many times to ensure the ideas would catch on.

It's not as though we didn't *know* about those things, Ilse wanted to burst out sometimes. We just didn't *talk* about them endlessly. She and her husband and their friends had been children during the Holocaust, after all, and the atom bomb; they'd lost fathers to Normandy and the Pacific. It's not as though horrible things were new. But she said nothing, content to sigh audibly and shift in her chair and roll her eyes at Maisie Williamson, who would, head ducked, grin covertly back. These young things and their diatribes and their self-righteousness and their jeans. *We* wore jeans when they were called dunga-rees, when it meant something. Oh, well. Each generation had to discover its own stupidity.

Like sex. Each generation had to discover it afresh and go around acting like they'd invented fire. It was 1957 when she and Tom had settled into their little home on their little street; later, they'd had to read about the flower children and women say-ing yes to men who said no in the newspapers and *Life*, because the sexual revolution hadn't very much visited Halford. She remembered wondering why all the fuss. When she and Tom had discovered it, they hadn't rushed into the streets to pro-claim it. They'd simply done it and done it and done it, privately, nightly, and assumed everyone else was quietly partaking of it as well, and that's what led people to secretly smile sometimes, and that's what it meant to be grown up. When she and Tom had discovered it—

But here were the first ladies coming now, joining together in pairs in the street as they got from their cars and walking up the walk as in a procession. And yes, they were pausing just under the pergola to point and admire. Ilse sighed with satisfaction. The sun shone, the linoleum gleamed, the stacked china cups winked from the sideboard. Everything was perfect. She untied the strings of her apron and lifted it over her head with a little groan—her shoulders, too, sometimes ached—and hung it on its hook with satisfaction: her flower-sprigged dress was still immaculate. She slipped on her summer-weight cashmere car-digan, pale primrose, to conceal the loose winging flesh of her forearms, poor things, and smoothed her hair as she passed the hall mirror. The bell rang.

And everything went perfectly: the flurry of greetings and com-pliments on her décor, the settling into chairs, everyone finding a comfortable place, the reading of the minutes, of a letter from a member summering in Sweden, of the announcements, of the paper on Barbara Kingsolver, and then afterwards the nice discussion, everything happily oiled and leavened by the fond glances from one friend to another. And then everyone rose and there were the effusions of thanks and again compliments on her house and her dress and the pretty little decorated biscuits, and happy chatter about upcoming summer vacations and grandchildren's graduations and when they'd be off to college. Even the amount of cream in the little pitcher was perfect; she hadn't needed to leave the living room to refill it. And then eventually came the tapering in volume, the quick light hand on her arm, the thanks and smiles and goodbyes, some cheek-kisses, and she could see through the hall window that little knots of women were still standing about on the front patio, gesturing toward the wisteria and the little wrought iron table and chairs and the large glossy ceramic pots full of zinnias. She hoped, she willed them to stay, young and old and middle-aged, talking and gesturing with admiration, so that they'd be visible for as long as possible from all up and down the straight little tree-lined street, so that her neighbors would see she'd had some kind of party, and all her guests dressed so gaily, too, in such distinguished pretty clothes and calling goodbye to one another in low cultivated tones and getting into cars that could never embarrass anyone. Those were the kinds of friends she had.

She closed the door behind the last guest and the house seemed to sigh happily with her as she turned to gaze upon the disarrayed folding chairs, the trash of wadded pink paper napkins and smeared plates strewn across the sideboard and coffee table, all of it still seeming to quiver and hum with the energy of the lovely gracious ladies who were her friends and near acquaintances, though she did not, it's true, know some of them well.

She gathered up some dishes, stacking them, gripping them carefully with fingers she knew to be treacherously unpredictable in their sudden bouts of weakness, and headed toward the kitchen. She'd considered asking Antoinette to come but had decided against it, wanting to enjoy instead the private pleasure of cleaning up after something wonderful in order to savor it, the way as a teenager she'd slipped down early on Saturday mornings after her parents had hosted a dinner or cocktail party the night before, one she and her brother and sisters would have been sent upstairs for, and she'd revel in cleaning up alone, soaking the crystal wine glasses with their thick maroon scum like the very promise of adulthood, humming "La Vie en Rose" and "Que Sera, Sera," imagining she was in a garret in Montparnasse or the Latin Quarter cleaning up after her own wild, bohemian party while her lover (a tumbling-haired painter of bold, arresting canvases) slept, and she moved through their tiny apartment—no, atelier—on the wingéd feet of love. She remembered all that now, feeling a similar rush of pleasure. Only now this was real. A girl growing up on a perfectly ordinary street in St. Paul, she had sweetened her housework by dreaming of Paris. She'd never made it to Petra or Alexandria or Istanbul, places in the picture books she'd mooned over. How had a girl like that ended up planted in Halford? But she had.

Wellesley had been the pinnacle of her adventure, really, and meeting Tom. Once when he'd been in graduate school and they'd lived in the little married student apartments in Billings, she'd thrown a Come As Your Madness costume party, after Anaïs Nin's, and the other would-be biologists and their wives had seemed nervous and shocked and then had rather enjoyed it. But that was all, really: the extent of it. She had come to Halford, had her happy life with Tom, and then grown old.

Ilse laughed aloud, not a mocking laugh derisive of her younger self or a laugh bitter with life's swift passing or anything like that, but a soft, fond laugh that partook of the pleasure of the moment, of seeing everything and not minding, of cleaning up after a perfectly ordinary meeting of the Ladies' Literary Society as the late sun poured through the French doors, the polished panes of which showed the pretty backyard with its long slope of lawn that unrolled like a smooth carpet down to the Souris River. This was real life, and it was lovely. Birdsong once again filled the house. In the kitchen, she set the plates on the counter, and another sound reached her.

"I know. Jesus. I thought it would never end." It was the low voice of a young woman, and another low voice laughed. Ilse froze. They were right beneath the window.

"I mean, maybe it was relevant once, you know, when none of them had jobs or anything and all they did was take care of kids all day."

"Yeah, back then they probably had to give papers just to remember they even had brains." Nearly all the parked cars were gone from the street.

"Well, I can't handle it. An afternoon off work every month for this crap?"

"I know! Exactly! I mean, I analyze stuff all day. On deadline. This isn't my idea of *fun*."

"I know, right? And a tea party? It's all so genteel, it's bizarre."

"I know. I totally want to quit, but how? It would be so awkward."

"I know. Me, too." There was a pause and a clearing of a throat. "But you do feel so touched, you know, being asked, and they *are* really sweet."

The other one made a gagging sound. "Sweet and geriatric."

"But what else are you going to do in a pit like Halford?"

"I know. These things are the barometer of exactly how pathetic my social life has become." They laughed throatily and moved off across the lawn.

From the back, Ilse could see who they were, and she felt a delicate, horrible shock. They were, she had once thought, such nice young women. She had voted *yes* to induct them two years ago. The one with the long auburn ponytail and black pantsuit was a new professor at the university, in history, and the slimmer one with short dark hair and a peasant skirt had moved here for her husband's job but did things on her computer for an environmental group in the Twin Cities. They waved to each other, got in their cars, and drove away.

Ilse leaned on tiptoe to look down over the windowsill to where they'd been standing. The heels of their shoes had left dark stab-holes in the grass, and petal-shards were scattered everywhere. The house felt very still and pressurized suddenly, as though air were being forced into it from somewhere. Those young women had stood there, talking, absently shredding her flowering clematis.

Her breath, she realized, was coming fast in little gasps: she was panting. In a daze she left the mess and wandered to the French doors at the back of the house and stood there, looking out, away from the street and hidden from it, one hand on the handle and one hand on the center of her chest. A loud buzz sounded hotly in her ears. She pushed the curved brass s-handle down and out, and the cool smell of cut grass rushed in at her. This would not rattle her. This was merely an overheard insignificance. Those were the subjective views of other people, of foolish young women.

Standing on the flagstones just outside, she held onto the

open door for support, the closed door still latched steadily into place, secure, and she stepped out of her elegant low-heeled pumps. Through her stockings came the damp cold shock of stone. Something was buzzing at the edge of her memory, and she reached up under her dress to her waist with both hands and rolled the pantyhose down. She suddenly had a fierce, bizarre need to get the constriction away from her skin. No one could see. The yard was fenced on both sides, and across the river were only woods. And even if someone did see, what matter? A crazy old lady taking her clothes off? She held onto the door again to slide first one foot and then the other from the nylon, which she dropped in a little heap next to her shoes. It lay there, unsightly and rumpled, flesh-colored, faintly embarrassing, like the shed shell of a cicada. What *was* she trying to remember?

She stepped barefoot into the grass, and its cool freshness shot up through her: the smooth lawn, groomed by Tom for years, was so shaded the grass felt almost wet, even in late afternoon after a day of sun. The backyard had been a point of pride for him, something they enjoyed together in private. One could, if one wanted, lie down at the top and roll down its long gentle slant right to the river without incurring a single scratch or bump. One night they had done just that, in the moonlight, in the snow, all bundled up in their waterproof insulated clothes, giggling, and the next morning they'd laughed together at the wide twin tracks to the ice and made up imaginary snow-creatures with Latin names that could have left them. Thirty years ago or more. *Emotion recollected in tranquility* flashed suddenly into her mind, but that wasn't what she was trying to think of. It's what Wordsworth had said about poetry, and it occurred to her that all she'd had, for years now, was tranquility and recollection. A woman's longer life span was nothing to be envied. She walked slowly through the grass toward the water as though feeling her way through a dark house at night.

Ah, there it was. A story. It had been sometime during the 1960s, yes, and the Society had met at Julia Richards' house, with its mod pillows shipped direct from New York, to discuss the stories of Katherine Mansfield. In those days, they'd all read the book in advance and could ask informed questions, not like today. People had had more time then and felt more responsible. Those Mansfield stories were wonderful—perhaps, as the presenter had noted, only minor rather than great, but very wonderful, and Ilse had loved them. Amidst all the stories of bohemian fresh young things falling in and out of love, which she had loved the most, and stories of precocious children who sensed deep truths, and everything having symbolic resonance and epiphanies and the losses of innocence, there had been one old-lady story. In the 1960s, she'd paid it little mind.

But now it came back to her. The main character had been an old lady, an aging spinster, a tutor of some kind, dressed up and sitting in the park on a sunny day and seeing everyone suddenly as part of life's great pageant, all acting together in a beautiful romantic play or opera, and herself proudly perched on the bench in her little old fur, dressed up for her part—a bit part, admittedly, but a part nonetheless, a role that mattered; just her witnessing, appreciating presence mattered—with her fox tippet much repaired but lovingly brushed and fairly shooting out gleams of elegance, everything marvelous and this little old lady swimming in her wondrous apprehension of wholeness and radiance and belonging. Ilse remembered it all now.

And then the boy and girl had appeared at the end of the bench, young lovers eager for privacy who said rash careless casual things about her—Miss Brill! that was it, and Mercy Putnam, who gave the paper, had explained that *brill* meant a small fish but also might mean brilliant, but of what significance that was, Ilse could not recall—the couple said those casual cutting things about Miss Brill loudly enough for her to hear, not because they were cruel but because they were oblivious and young and full of their own desires. And all the old lady's vision of radiant harmony folded at once like a tent collapsing, and Miss Brill folded herself up and walked home to her small apartment and closed herself in and put the fur away in its box, reassuring herself bravely that all had been well, that the day had been fine, that young people will simply be *young*, that's all. But as she stored the box away—Ilse thought she could recall it now, decades later, almost word for word—as she put it back up on its shelf, Miss Brill thought she heard the sound of something crying.

And that was all. That was the end. That was Mansfield's genius, to say it and get away clean, leaving it hovering there— perhaps not true genius, perhaps only minor genius or a gift, to be sure. Ilse, slowing her descent to the river, remembered the story clearly now. The cold damp made the bones in her feet ache more keenly than usual, but the wind rushed through the leaves overhead with a beautiful sound and shushed against her face. Lovely.

There would be the sound of nothing crying here. Those girls and their casual sneers would not trouble her. Remembering the story gave her sustenance, made her determined to not, herself, inhabit the role of a defeated old lady with all her pleasure punctured, a cliché imaginable by some young minor writer-girl, however clever, who died of TB at thirty-four. To hell with young girls and their pantsuits. She refused to be a cliché, to be imaginable, to be punctured. And the Ladies' Literary Society itself had done that for her. Books and reading had fortified her. And she had learnt that thing about Miss Brill alone, with a book, reading, not in company with people discussing. Just by herself with a book. But then, she conceded, she might not have read that particular book at all if the Text Selection Committee had not chosen it that year. There was value in being assigned things.

She shook the pain off. Caught by surprise she might have been, but not caught entirely unaware. Katherine Mansfield had spared her that. She would be richer, stronger than little Miss Brill, and she cast about in her mind for a way to be so.

Say, perhaps, that Halford *was* a pit, and a cold pit at that: each winter some poor old fool doddered out in a blizzard and died twelve feet from the front door, and she'd often wondered if that would be how she'd go, disoriented and frozen. Halford was an unforgiving place. And perhaps her life did amount to just so much nothing, as the girls had implied. She didn't even have the excuse of children, just herself and Tom, and every summer the flowers and traveling for his collecting trips and years of reading wonderful books, hundreds and hundreds of them. The romance of a biologist was an odd thing, too, perhaps not what one dreamed of as a girl: "You have the prettiest ears," he'd once whispered, holding her, "of any creature of your species." It was all perhaps terribly small, really, and she saw it suddenly and clearly as the girls must see it, very small and very far away, inconsequential.

Suddenly she saw herself like an ant in a colony or a bee in a hive, industriously getting along with all the other bugs—how Tom would have chided her, calling them *bugs* instead of *insects*, and she smiled—trying to conceal anything about her own little wax pod that might seem alarmingly *different*, might make the others turn on her, attack her or shun her. She wondered which would hurt more: being shredded and devoured, or the silence of turned backs. Or both: she imagined the most vicious of them—Lydia from church with the rigid hair, or that snippy bow-tied classics professor, who seemed to hate everyone born after Christ, and women especially: he thought them all simply dumb. She could tell by the way he never bothered to look in her eyes but was always gazing about the room for someone more intelligent. He had once abandoned her mid-sentence—his own—to read the back label of a pale-blue bottle of Bombay Sapphire Gin. They were the most vicious, and she imagined them ripping into her, their multifaceted eyes glittering, their slavering jowls, etc., while the gentler, soberer ones, eager to remain uneaten, ascribed the blame to her and quietly closed ranks. Oh, how often she had longed to be just a hobbit in her hobbit-hole, tucked away, satisfied with little comforts and treats.

But this was fanciful. She was getting self-indulgent. Living in community was perhaps problematic, perhaps complicated, but she was no hobbit, no bug.

She had reached the river, and she placed her feet in the silt and watched the water run over her pale skin and purply knots. The ache of the cold was bitter, but she lowered herself slowly backward, cautiously cantilevering her bottom down to the grass at the water's edge. The sunlight turned the water gold where it struck, and in shadow it was pewter.

In the old days they'd all worn bow ties and tweed, even Tom. Now you could tell who felt besieged by the new, who missed the dear old comfortable definitions and the days when men were men, etc., and the certainty of Shakespeare as indisputably great rather than the lucky subject of various ages' constructions of his meanings and so on. These shorers of fragments wore their bow ties and premature paunches and tweed like a badge of staunch struggle, like signs by which they could be recognized among the nations, and Ilse felt it odd that although she agreed with them on many things and found herself often longing, too, for the comfort of the old definitions, she could not like them very much. Sometimes even very young men wore those things, like those shouting fellows on television, and she wanted to take them aside and give them normal young men's clothes and pat their cheeks and say, *Now darling*, as when mothers gently untied the capes and took the plastic swords away so their overexcited boys could settle down and get ready for bed. But to see them and their shouting in that way was to simplify and condescend, she knew, and they were dangerous, they made wars, and surely there must be something more worthwhile and complex in their views. But she had listened and could not find it.

The Souris was a rippling, calm, unfazed river, a river she had watched as it swelled and ebbed and kept flowing at the edge of her property for upwards of forty years. Steadily there, beautifully flowing and freezing and thawing. Changing but there. She wanted to crawl into that metaphor as into a dry shelter, but to rely on that as if it meant something, she knew, was an illusion. She watched the news; she knew about climate change and terrible hurricanes and drought and the end of known things. You couldn't go around wantonly making symbols out of nature just to have something to hang onto; rivers could become irreversibly polluted or dry up at their source. She reached out and touched the water's cool skin with her fingertips. Rivers were vulnerable, too. It filled her with sudden anguish. What mattered now would one day no longer count, the lines of maps would be redrawn, and the life she'd built looked stupid to other people. What could one lone person do? How then must we live? That was Tolstoy.

She thought of those girls and their glossy thick locks that they'd never yet tugged side to side in the mirror, wondering if they looked too scalpy. There was so much they hadn't suffered yet, didn't know, the erosions of physical dignity, the loss forever of true love. It filled her with a kind of tenderness, the vast regions of what they didn't know yet. They were just idiots, she thought kindly. It wasn't their fault. Her life did seem tiny, microscopic, but it didn't sicken or appall her.

No, there was no sound of crying here. She wiggled her aching toes in the river. She would herself *be* something to hang onto. She would call those girls and invite them to lunch, and she wouldn't make delicate lady-sandwiches in triangles with the crusts cut away but the real sort of sandwiches she ate alone, thick slabs of everything: turkey, tomatoes, the homemade bread itself thickly cut, and plenty of grainy mustard and real mayonnaise. Something to wrap both hands around, to bite into. She could ask them about their loneliness. She could talk in ways not excessively polite but just real. Dozens of years and the Information Age need not separate human souls. She had been lonely, too, in Halford, when they'd first arrived.

Perhaps they would never think of her as anything better than old and sweet, but you can only control what you do, not what others think you are. Suddenly, she wondered what Antoinette thought of her. She had wondered that before, and carefully tidied away private or dirty things before the girl arrived; Antoinette cleaned other houses in the neighborhood, and she didn't want her talking. But what did Antoinette think about when *not* thinking about her? She had never even wondered. How extraordinary. She would ask. Perhaps she would make Antoinette that sort of sandwich and set down two plates on the kitchen table, and ask something benign, inconsequential, at first, so as not to make her shy, and then listen. They had never eaten together.

Perhaps what one lone person could do was to forgive. To not be like the land, like the world, pitiless and unreliable, but instead be steady and true and kind.

At this, her throat cramped up, muscular and hot, and her failing eyes burned with a sudden generous dampness, and she knew she had found it. Her body always confirmed an idea when it was right, like a bell being struck.

Steady and true and kind, then. Not a particularly glamorous thing, perhaps, but something.

The wet brimming of unshed tears made everything clear for a moment, and her vision sharpened so she could see into the woods across the river. The rough bark of quite distant trees leapt into view. Each twig was crisply etched against the light. How strangely visible everything was. She knew the woods went on for a long way, but it seemed as though she could see more deeply into them than she ever had before.

A Choice I Made

This falling-down house on the west side of San Antonio cost me six thousand dollars at auction. All my savings—years of waiting tables and odd jobs—bought a foreclosure in a barrio near Our Lady of the Lake University.

In terms of the long view, this house is a tenuous enterprise. In ancient Egypt, they had a dynasty system that lasted nearly three thousand years, from 2700 B.C. until the Romans defeated Cleopatra. I saw this on PBS with my girls. By comparison, our attempt at self-rule is new. Two other single moms and all seven of our kids and me have been living in this reject house for only five months. It's no dynasty. But hey, it's a peaceable kingdom so far.

It's a one-story wooden house, pier-and-beam, with three bedrooms, one bath, and window units, and when you try not to think about fancy houses in magazines—when you think instead of twelve South Africans living in a tin shack, or of the train car your uncles came over in, flesh pressed to flesh, lungs quietly competing for limited air—then the ten of us here all spread out through the house, with doors and running water, seems like luxury.

"But no cable," I told Tisha and Sylvia right at the beginning: "We don't need to be seeing no lifestyles of the rich and famous." PBS has a lot of interesting stuff, though, so we try to keep it tuned to that. If we see the kids watching the Brady

Bunch or the Huxtables, we turn it off. All those pretty dreams went wrong for us, and we don't want our kids learning them. This is the house of making it up from scratch.

I want to be, God knows, a better person than I am. I want to be a fun mom. I have all these warm, friendly, fuzzy ideals that come to me in colors like cobalt and gold: visions of how I never get pissed off, and I'm always there when the kids get home, and I wipe the trashcan out with disinfectant on a rag every time I empty the garbage. In my visions I am kind and wise and clean, I listen attentively and say deep, peaceful stuff like the mom in the *Little Women* video, and I wake the kids up at night to lie in the backyard and watch meteor showers, and it's like an adventure and we're all whispery and giggly on the blanket.

The truth is that I'm tired a lot and cranky. My shifts on the Riverwalk last until midnight. Sylvia, Tisha, and me take turns watching each other's kids, and if it's me when everyone gets home from school, I nod and smile and make macaroni and cheese while listening to stories of seven separate days, pre-K through eighth grade. They're good kids, all of them, and I nod and stir things in the kitchen and ask meaningful questions about their day, and we all laugh together, but inside I'm groggy and bored.

My six-thousand-dollar house, pale green, paint peeling, nothing up to code, contains mi vida: my two girls, twelve and fourteen now, bouncing like little kids on the mattresses we found on curbs and hauled home tied to the top of my Mercedes. We bleached the hell out of them and laid them in the backyard and hosed them off. When the Texas sun had scorched them dry, we laid them longways end to end around the edges of the big living room, sheeted with garage-sale sheets, laundered and sweet-smelling, ready for Tisha's and Sylvia's children, too:

seven skinny mattresses edging the room, their stains concealed under flowers and sailboats, and we hung the kids' paintings from art class on the mango-colored walls. The kids love it. It's like a permanent sleepover.

And Tisha and Sylvia were shocked and touched at having their own personal rooms—like me, for the first time ever. The little cardboard sign in the hall, hand-lettered in black magic marker in fancy gothic letters, says, "SOLEDAD=SANITY." They had assumed each little family would be crammed into one of the three bedrooms, but no, sir. We were grown. How could we respect ourselves when we'd never had a door to close?

My own room was quiet, the stripped cell of a nun, clean even of color, waiting for the day when prettiness or mirrors or thick shining fabrics might seem desirable again, when scented candles and flowers and small pretty objects on a shelf might feel like reasonable things to add to a life. For now, my rosary hung on a whitewashed wall, and La Virgen was tacked to the back of my door. It was her kind, sad eyes avoiding mine that I saw before I fell asleep.

"The thing is, Iréne," mi madre would say, "you're not a stupid girl. Not like your cousins, thanks be to God. You're a smart girl. School-smart, book-smart." This, because I made As in schools that were failing; I would never have made it in Olmos Park or Alamo Heights. But Mami just saw the As. "But you have no people-smarts, no, so you throw it all away, ya veras—" She'd shake her head so as not to utter the end of the sentence: on those pretty-boy machos who don't give a damn about your heart, m'ija. Who never learned respeto.

Yes, Mami. Guess you'd know. But I didn't say that, either.

"You could make a success of your life, child," she said, "if you tried. You always had nothing but energy, God knows."

No cable, no drugs, no men in the house overnight, no children left without adult supervision, and each woman had her own key. Those were our simple rules. All bills would get split three ways, equally, no matter how many kids a woman had. The word *solidarity* was new to me, but I loved saying it.

We all paid for our own phones, though. I thought up that part since I didn't want to get burned by some three-hundred-dollar phone bill when I don't even know nobody outside San Anto. All my people are local. The night a year ago when Raul threw me out of his car near downtown—swerved into a parking lot, leaned over to open the door and push me out, said, "Get your own ride, fucking mouthy bitch," and drove away in the dark—I knew six phone numbers right off I could call, all within five miles, people with cars, or at least people who could borrow somebody's car to come get me.

But I was embarrassed to call anyone. I stood there in my party dress and little shoes, hanging tight to my handbag and thinking, *Okay, okay, no hay problema, stick your finger down your throat and puke if anyone stops to mess with you, now which way is it to Tito's?* Then out of nowhere the engine roared, and Raul pulled up again, laughing, and leaned across the front seat and pushed open the passenger door.

"Get in," he yelled. In the backseat, his friend was laughing, too, but the girl looked through the window at me with dark still eyes. "I was just fucking with you, hey? Get in."

Her expression was pale and serious, like she knew the stakes, like she'd stood alone before, dumped in a dark parking lot, wondering what next. Her black eyeliner flowed in fluid, stark lines and swung up like little wings.

"Hey, Iréne, get the fuck in!"

She looked at me. She knew that another night, it could be her.

"You retarded, bitch?" Raul yelled, waving his arm. "Get your ass in the car!"

There was a moment then, when things seemed to stop, when I wavered, when I stood on the brink of something and could have gone either way. I stood draped in the white blanket of the security lights, staring at Raul's mouth, which kept yelling in slow motion.

In Version A, what could have happened is that I got in the car, because what else could I do? Raul drove to the party, and we all drank too much and got high, and the girl and me never looked at each other all night, and I never saw her again, and after a while Raul and me broke up and now I'm with some other guy.

But in Version B, the girl's door opened, too, and she got out into the cooling dark air.

"I'm Tisha," Her voice was little-girl high. She shut both car doors at once. Raul glowered up through the windshield. The rectangle of the lot was washed white with lights, but outside the perimeter, it was dark.

"Couple of crazy fucking putas," he said in his about-to-hit-someone voice. I could read his lips and I could hear him, muffled, through the glass. "You crazy fucking cunts." But his friend in the backseat slapped his shoulder, still laughing, and said something, and vaulted like liquid into the front seat. The car squealed off with that I'm-a-man, I'm-a-righteous-pissed-off-man grind of gears and brakes and gas at once.

I knew it well. It was a sound guys had used on me since high school, the sound of owning the power of machines, the power to leave or run you down, and it always did the trick of scaring me into whatever they wanted, me who'd had to keep scraping up quarters for Via until I was thirty and finally bought my car, and even then I still seemed to find myself in the passenger seat with the men I dated. Like I'd just handed them the keys.

The sound of Raul's engine faded, and then it was just regular tame traffic going by, weeknight downtown traffic, and there were two of us, no longer just one woman, not a target dressed up in pretty party clothes alone.

We stood in the vast, empty square of light. The parking lot was like a big, blank sheet of paper, with our bodies and shadows the only writing on it. We could move in any direction we chose. In the distance, I could see the neon sign on top of the Tropicana. I tried to get my bearings.

"I've got some cousins around here," I said, looking down a dark street. "I think they live that way."

"We'll find them," she said, and we started walking. The houses were small, the yards little. Behind chain-link fences, fiberglass Virgins smiled down at patchy grass. Dogs lunged suddenly at us from their dark yards, barking and snarling, their claws hooking in the mesh of chain-link when they leaped. After a block, Tisha took my arm, and after a few more steps, she turned her head and gave me a tiny smile. It had a little curl of something tough. There was more to her than I'd thought when we'd stopped to pick her up in the dusk and she'd baby-stepped out to the car like a doll.

My arm held to the heat of her ribs felt good, and I suddenly laughed. Then we were both laughing, laughing so hard we were bent over, laughing like the crazy with our hands on our shins. Hot tears squeezed from my eyes. Down from the branches filtered the soft, sweet scent of mimosas, and I was gasping so hard I could taste their pink blossoms.

When we could, we stood up straight again, gasping and wiping our eyes. We linked our arms a little tighter and kept walking together up the dark street.

GRATITUDE

Many thanks to my lovely, funny editor, Kristen Elias Rowley, who made this book possible, and to my wonderful agent, Mitchell Waters, and his assistant, Steven Salpeter. Many thanks to everyone who has read and offered feedback on these stories over the years, especially Ewing Campbell, Heather Lundine, Lorraine M. López, and my husband, James MacDougall. The unforgettable lesson Paul D. taught Sethe was that she, and not her child, Beloved, was her own best thing. Yet somewhere in my heart skulks the suspicion that—for me, at least—Morrison is wrong, that my son, Grey, truly is my very best thing. The world's best gift to me, and my best gift to the world. These stories would not exist without him.

In "Independence Day" the line "Nobody, nobody, nobody, truly lives on earth" and the adapted lines "Now I was learning its truth in my flesh / Now I was going to the place of defleshing" are from Miguel Leon-Portilla and Earl Shorris's *In the Language of Kings: An Anthology of Mesoamerican Literature, Pre-Columbian to the Present*. "Independence Day" is based on historical research by Maythee Rojas in "Remembering Josefa: Reading the Mexican Female Body in California Gold Rush Chronicles," *Women's Studies Quarterly* 35 (2007): 126–48. In "The Small Heart" the following lines are from ZZ Packer's

"The Ant of the Self," in *Drinking Coffee Elsewhere*: "Outside, autumn is over, and yet it's not quite winter. Indiana farmlands speed past in black and white. Beautiful. Until you remember that the world is supposed to be in color."

Grateful acknowledgment is made to the following journals and anthologies, in which versions of these works originally appeared:

"A Notion I Took": *North American Review*
"Other Women's Jewels": *Puerto del Sol*
"Giving Jewel Away": *A Ghost at Heart's Edge: Stories and Poems of Adoption*
"To Practice the Thing": *Short Story*
"Liking It Rough": *Texas Review*
"Independence Day": *The Normal School*
"The Noren": *Puckerbrush Review*
"A Favor I Did": *Avery: An Anthology of New Fiction*
"How Winter Began": *Angels of the Americlypse: An Anthology of New Latin@ Writing*
"Whore for a Day": *Afro-Hispanic Review*
"Dinner": *Grasslands Review*
"The River": *Platte River Review*

To order or obtain more information on these or other University of Nebraska Press titles, visit nebraskapress.unl.edu.

CPSIA information can be obtained at www.ICGtesting.com
Printed in the USA
LVOW10s1111240815

451299LV00001B/37/P